Published 2005
Printed in the United States of America

ISBN 1-933570-73-3

51300

9 781933 570730

www.lenamiddleton.com

True Divas

True Divas

Written by: Lena L. Middleton
Contributors: TonyWHOA-5th Eye Entertainment,
A.D. Wallace II, Shenika A. Moses-Public Relations,
Linda & Anthony Wallace I, and Eric L. Middleton-Photography

Acknowledgements

First and most importantly, I would like to thank the Lord. For through him all things are possible. Next, I would like to thank Eric, my best-friend, my back bone, my rock, the father of my children, and most importantly my husband.

I would like to thank my parents, Anthony I and Linda, and my big head brother, Tony Whoa! We will always be the "Awesome Foursome"! I would like to thank my "other" mother, Brenda Crayton and my sis-in-law Tanisha Middleton for welcoming me into the family like I was born in. I would like to thank my great-grandmother, Lena, for with out you I would have no name.

...And last, but most definitely not least, I would like to thank my girlfriends, the REAL True Divas; Shenika, Marquita, Crystal/Duchess, and Candice. You ladies are the sisters I never had, and the women who helped me realize every woman needs her GIRLFRIENDS!

Love you all,
Lena

Lu Lu

"Girl, pull yourself together, the limo will be there at nine o'clock sharp, and you better be ready. Stop worrying about a damn fire, the fire department would have cited us if it was a problem. I'm getting off the phone, goodbye!"

That heffah is crazy. She is so worried about how she might die that she can't even live. Will I drown, will I burn, will I die in a car crash. Good grief! She makes me worry. I'm gonna have to get her out of the house more often. She obviously needs a man.

It was about fifteen years ago when I met my two best friends, my home girls, my sistah sistah (snap snap) girlfriends. Both of the heffah's drive me insane, but I couldn't live without either one of them. They are the only sisters I have being an only child. And the only other women I can deal with.

Trust me, I would much rather hang with a group of men then a group of whining, conniving, jealous, stuck up ass women.

I'm just being honest, I mean I know I got it going on and jealousy from other women is inevitable. That's why I like Gabby and Deja, they got it going on as tough as I do. ***True diva's*** is what I like to call us. I'm still the same size I was in high school, just with a little more hips and tits. I don't mean to toot my own horn, but you know how it is...beep beep.

Now don't get my wrong; my girls do have their issues. Poor Gabby, I didn't realize how crazy her ass was until I saw her sitting in the audience on the Montel Williams show. She was listening to that woman go on about how she talks to the dead. You should've seen her crazy ass, eyes as wide as the sun soaking it all in.

However, home girl is as fine as wine and has most men slobbering at the mouth. Gabby has caramel brown skin with long jet black hair. Her hair and body is a blessing and a curse. Most men love her because she has a shape like an hour glass, perfectly proportioned, and she has very long hair. Most women hate her, one because her body is perfect and two because her hair is real. No weave. Then there is my girl Deja. Deja is the only married one out of the click, but she can hang just as tough as we do. Her hubby, David, is a corporate guru and always traveling, so we keep her company most of the time. But don't get it twisted, Deja loves her some David, and David loves him some Deja.

Oh yeah, and she's fine too. Deja is our high yellow sistah, or as brotha's say, "she's a red bone". She has that naturally curly hair, and she wears shoulder length in what she calls a natural. But many sistah's would have to pay money to get a look like that. She's beautiful, picture perfect without make-up. Many a player has tried to play Raphael Sideeq and sing her a song like that movie "Higher Learning", but Deja ain't hearing it, she loves her man, and takes her marriage vows very seriously.

Finally, there's me, LuLu. I'm the relaxed one. I just like to hang out and have fun. It takes a lot to ruffle my feathers, but don't cross me, when it comes to my money or my career because I will cut you deep. I am the youngest Marketing Manager at Roche Molecular Inc, not to mention the only black one. I have to wear a thick skin at all times.

I'm the chocolate sistah. I love my complexion. Kids used to tease me about it growing up, but I knew back then I was beautiful. I keep my hair as short as possible. I've become known for my short-do's, and my beautician, April over at Verse A Stylez, keeps my do looking fresh each week. And I might add that my body is banging. Once again, I'd hate to toot my own horn, but a sistah knows when she looks good.

Today is the big day, the grand opening of *True Divas*. *True Divas* is our new club named solely after my girls and me. I'm so excited. Diva's was actually Gabby's idea, but as always, she came up with a million and two reasons why it was a risk to start a club. She wouldn't go through with it, so I did. We all put in a lot of hard work to get to this day.

Now Gabby's dream is finally a reality.

We designed the club together from front to back, and top to bottom. When you walk in the front door, the first thing you see is a life size portrait of the true divas. Yep you guessed it, me and my girls looking fly and living large. As I was saying, tonight is the grand opening. I hope everything goes well. I used every last connection I had in order to pull this off. There will be local media camera crews, radio stations, and the whole nine yards. This will be the shit. I know it will. This will be the hottest club in Indy, Lord knows we need one.

Gabby

I really don't want to go to the grand opening tonight, but it was my idea. I'm not sure the space is large enough. Maybe LuLu should have searched for a larger building. I mean, what if there's a fire? How in the hell will we all get out of there alive? I just know I can't burn to death. Just my luck, I would live and ninety percent of my body would be covered in burns. Oh Lord, just give me strength.

I've tried three different outfits, and finally decided on the perfect one. It's a two piece ivory pants suit. I decided to go for the sophisticated lady look. There will be enough hoochies dressing that part.

There's a single button on the jacket, just enough space to show the "girls" off with just the right push up bra. And the shoes I have to go with it, woo, three and a half inch man killers is what I like to call them. This outfit will surely take my mind off the disasters that could happen.

I may even find my future husband at the opening. Although, they say it's not good to meet a man in a club. I'll just have to see, I mean, if he's tall, dark, and lovely like Morris Chestnut, all rules and reasoning will go right out the window. That's my problem; I have a weakness for dark chocolate.

I would love to have what Deja has with David. A true love and best friend wrapped up into one. I love her to death, but jealousy is always a motha sucka. I mean damn, I'm fine too, but somehow I've become a dog magnet. It's like a wear a damn kibbles and bits necklace.

The men I attract are fine, sexy, educated, and have good jobs, but they always turn out to be a bonefied D.O.G. Just trying to get me in the bed, turn a sistah out, don't want me, but don't want anybody else to have me type brothers.

I swear if Diva's doesn't take off, I'm leaving Indy. There can't be any good men left here, can't be. Shit, I want a husband and a baby, and I don't have time to wait until I'm forty. I mean, isn't that when women are at risk for having babies with Down Syndrome? Oh no, that's one more thing I have to worry about.

Deja

I'm so proud of LuLu for making Gabby's dream a reality. We all helped, but my girl LuLu did most of the work. The club is truly a reflection of all three of us, the true divas. I gotta give my girl her props, she's crazy, but she has deep connections and some serious business savvy.

David would kill me if he saw the outfit I'm wearing to the grand opening. I know I'm married, but he travels so much, and a sistah has to feel like she's still got it, and I do still have it.

I've been through my closet, LuLu's and Gabby's, but I still had to go to the mall. I do believe I've mastered the art of shopping. I settled on this black dress, I should say THEE black dress. It's cut down the tailbone in the back and the navel in the front. I know it's a tease, but like I said, a sistah needs a little attention now and then. And the shoes, oh the shoes. The shoes will get attention on their own, three and a half inch heels with straps all the way up the calf. Gabby calls them "man killers". Not to mention I just got the most invigorating French pedicure one could imagine. I had to make sure the toes were looking nice and summarized.

I love to be pampered. I guess that's why I shouldn't complain about David traveling so much. It allows me to do the things that Deja likes to do. As a teacher, I wouldn't make enough money alone to have weekly pedicures and such, but I love my bad ass kids. I teach third grade at Greenwood Academy. It's a wonderful new charter school in the heart of the projects. Most of the kids attend on vouchers, but I wouldn't have it any other way. The kid's education shouldn't suffer because their parents are struggling. Third graders are hilarious too; you wouldn't believe the crap that comes out of their mouths.

I can't wait to get to the club. Normally, I'm not one for clubbing it, especially when David's not in town, but this is different. This is "our" big night, my girls and I.

Diva's Grand Opening
Deja

"Yes, this is high class. LuLu, you didn't tell us there would be a red carpet and everything! Gurrrl, I'm feeling like Jada Pinkett Smith over here"

"Deja, you are crazy, you know that right? But I love you anyway". Lu Lu laughed. "Calm down Gabby damn! You over there looking like you are about to freak out or something. What's wrong with you now?"

"Girl, I'm so clumsy, I just hope I don't trip over the carpet. You know it's a job to walk in these heels. They are sitting shoes, not walking shoes". Gabby whined.

"You'll be fine. Just move your hips and sashay on down

that red carpet. I am so excited. Lu Lu, make sure they keep those cameras off me. Shoot, I'm trying to get my groove on tonight, and I don't want David having a coronary when he gets back from Korea. He said he was going to check us out on-line since you hired that promo company to use the party cam on the Internet".

"Girl please, all you'll be doing is dancing, he can deal with that can't he?" Lu Lu said with a smirk on her face.

See, that is exactly what I'm talking about. First of all, these girls don't know a thing about being married. Secondly, all the understanding and the "I'll trust you alone in a room with a butt naked women named Halle Berry" shit is for the birds. Trust ain't that damn deep for anyone. Especially since David has had at least two affairs. Those are the two that I know about. Don't get me wrong, I love David, but ALL men are dogs. No matter how good you may think your man is, he's a damn dog too. That's just the way it is.

That's why I'm excited about the grand opening. It's our moment to shine, and I may find me a little piece of man candy to pass the time with.

I could never explain these feelings to my girls. I love them to death, but they would die if they knew I ever thought about cheating on David. They love him like a brother, not to mention we are their perfect vision of marriage and how it's supposed to be. Like I said before, they have no clue.

Only married sistah's can relate to what I'm rapping about. Don't get me wrong, I don't want to leave my husband; at least I don't think I do. I love him to death and I've never considered leaving before. I just want him to hurt the way he hurts me. The type of hurt that crushes your heart and physically makes you sick. I know, I know, that sounds terrible right? Maybe I need to pray on this one.

Gabby

Yes, this song is my jam! They are playing R. Kelley's "Step in the Name of Love". It's something about this song that makes you want to smile and get up on your feet. One thing about heels, man killers, it is easier to dance in them. Not to mention, I learned to step straight out of Chicago, so I got some moves Naptown knows nothing about.

And the man I'm steppin with, Malcolm, I believe, is as fine as wine. When he walked up to me, I almost started slobbering at the mouth. God has truly blessed this man. Woo! He is tall, caramel, and lovely. He's not my chocolate thunder, but he will most definitely do. The baldhead is definitely a plus.

"Look at you with LL Cool Jay's twin brother!" LuLu whispered in my ear. "Girl look at his arms, I just wanna grab them," she squealed as she stepped away.

"Oh no my sistah, you have to go get your own, this one is mine", I laughed as I turned to grind my backside into his stuff. The DJ started bumpin' Pherrell. This is my jam, I love this song. You can see everyone's mouth saying "hah, hah" with the song. It's perfect for what I'm trying to spring on this brotha. I know I'm moving just right because I can feel Mr. Malcolm start to rise, I guess I should turn around now. I shouldn't be a tease.

What's Deja doing over there in that corner sitting on that mans lap? That sure looks like that football player we knew in college. Humph, this is not a good sign.

Yes, that is him. He and Deja were like two dogs in heat back in the day. Yep, most definitely not a good sign.

Deja

I spotted his fine ass from half way across the room. I couldn't believe it. His name is Derrick Carter, and he went to State with my girls and me.

I didn't know what a real man was until he came along. I had been with my high school sweet heart for three years by the time I got to State, and was totally convinced that I was in love and getting married.

That was until I met Mr. Carter. He was a junior on the football team. There were billboards up and down the street, and posters everywhere with his pictures on it. He tried to holler at me for months. However, I'm not like most women, I wasn't impressed with all of his popularity. As a matter of fact, it turned me off because he thought he was the shit.

For months, I totally ignored him and all of his advances. I repeatedly told him that I loved my man, and I wasn't stupid, I knew a dog when I saw one. I was raised with three older brothers, and I wasn't about to fall for his so-called game.

He thought I was hilarious. He would always laugh at my comments, and never gave up. One night, my girls and I were invited to our first off campus football party, but we didn't have a car our freshman year. Of course Mr. Carter offered to pick us up, and we obliged.

We got to the party, and they were playing music I'd never heard before. However, I fell in love with it. House Music. The beat pumped so fast. I remember the words till this day "beat that bitch with a bat, beat that bitch with a bat"... I know it sounds vulgar, but we grew to love it. Mr. Carter asked me to dance, and I had no idea how to dance to this music. He told me it was a Chicago thing. I picked up quick, and began to pump my behind to the beat; it was so much fun. Next thing I knew, Derrick was down on the floor pumping with his mouth in my private area, I was so shocked. I was embarrassed and turned on all at the same time.

Needless to say, Derrick eventually wore me down. I called my high school sweetheart and dumped him over the phone, long distance, on his lunch break. Next thing I knew, this brotha drove all the way down to state from his army base, and was sitting outside my dorm room! I couldn't believe it! Gabby had to go console him because I truly did not care, at that point I didn't want him anymore.

This all occurred after Derrick took me back to my dorm after the party. I have a vivid memory of him making love to me with all my clothes on, and leaving because he didn't want to take advantage of me. Yeah right. He then came back an hour later stating he couldn't take it. He took all of my clothes off with his mouth and licked me from head to toe. I was in a state of pure shock.

I never knew cunnelingus was so pleasurable until I met this man. Next thing I knew, he had picked me up and made love to me right against my bedroom door. He worked it so slow and passionately even he began to cry. I loved Derrick Carter, and he loved me in return.

It was a weird kind of love though. It was the kind where we both knew a relationship would never work, not in that setting anyway. There were too many groupies, especially the rich white girls. They would do ANYTHING to get with a football player, and I do mean anything. I may have been young, but I was and always have been a realist. Remember my philosophy, all men are dogs anyway. Your daddy, your great granddaddy, and your uncles....they are all dogs. That's why I never allowed myself to get caught up in a relationship with Mr. Carter. State's football dream.

Well, we continued this way through my four years of college. He was a junior when I came, but he stayed at

State for grad school. I wouldn't take back a thing. Oh the memories.

As I spotted him across the room, he said, "Deja, Little Dee, it's so good to see you" he growled in that voice that he knows makes my panties melt off, ". And you still look good too, girl you are trying to hurt some niggas in a dress like that!" he smiled.

"It's really good to see you as well Mr. Carter, you're looking fine as always. So how's the football thing panning out?" I asked.

"It's cool, I like playing for the Colts so far, but I miss living and playing in Washington", he said as he stared off for a minute. "So, how's your husband?"

Humph, as if he really wanted to know. "He's fine, traveling as always. He's in Korea for the next few weeks. Not that you really care."

He smiled. "Touché. No, I don't really care how he's doing, but I would like to know if he's treating you okay."

Okay, momma always said you never tell another man your marital problems, but D and I go way back and a need a friend right now. I can't talk to LuLu or Gabby, and I don't want my family to look down upon David, so I can't tell them either.

I took a deep breath and said, "Well, actually things aren't going very well. I love David, but he has no idea what it means to be faithful. He treats me wonderfully when he's home, but while he's traveling, he can't seem to keep his dick in his pants. And that means most of the time because he travels 85% of the time".

Derrick laughed, "You know I know all about being a player, and I knew your dude was a smooth operator when I first met him. I could see the marks from his dog collar plain as day!" he laughed again, "I told you that Little Dee, but you thought I was just hatin".

"I know you told me that, but I thought things would change with marriage."

"But you know better than that Deja". He laughed again.

"Derrick, why do you keep laughing, I'm trying to be serious here, I'm really hurting".

He stroked my face lovingly, "It's not funny, I really feel bad. You know I would never treat you that way Deja, you know how I feel about you."

"What? How you feel about me?" I said shocked.

"Yes, how I feel about you. Dee, I've loved you since the first time I spoke to you. Remember me trying to holla at you that first day of class, you were crossing the street and I was rolling in my mini van bumbin with the football crew? You were the one that said it wasn't best for us to pursue a relationship in college, not me, remember?"

This man is so fine, and he looks so sincere. "Of course I remember, but there were so many women around you all the time. I just couldn't compete Derrick."

He frowned, "I never gave a fuck about anyone back at State but you, and I made that clear to you every night. When did I have time to be with other girls, Dee we were together every night? Even on curfew nights we were together.

He's right, but too much time has passed and I'm married now. But I can't help but feel the attraction to him. When I'm next to him, there's this invisible force of heat drawing me to him.

Here I am, in a club full of people and fine ass men, and I can only think of him. I want to be with him right here and right now. I want to make love to him, I want him to caress me and love me, just hold me.

LuLu

What the hell? Is that Derrick Carter? Uh oh. Deja has that look on her face. This is most definitely not a good sign.

See, my girl Deja may have Gabby fooled, but I know how it is. I know David has hurt my girl. Hell he called my crying because he thought Deja was going to kick his cheating ass out. I told him I didn't want anything to do with it, and although I loved him like a brother, he deserved whatever he got. Then he begged me not to tell Deja he called.

Men, they are so damn pathetic and predictable. That's why I'm single. Trust me, brothas have tried, but if it is one thing I can't stand, it's a no good lying ass brotha.

A man made me the way I am today. My girls think I am unloving, cold, and hardcore. They have no clue. I fell in love once. This was before I transferred to State and met my girls.

His name was Harold. I loved him with everything I had. One of my friends introduced me to him, and we hit it off right away.

They say you should always follow your first instinct, and instinct told me he and my friend were sleeping together, but I ignored it. I mean, if she wanted him, why would she introduce me to him? He was older, and so fine. He treated me like gold, bought me anything I asked for.

People told me things about him and the friend that introduced us, but I continued to ignore it. That is until one day, he stood me up. I was furious. I called up another one of my friends and had her high tale it to where I knew he would be. And sure enough, we pulled up to my "friends" house and there sat his red Cutlass Cierra. I could have screamed! It felt like someone punched me in the stomach.

I walked up and knocked on the door, and it took what felt like forever for her to answer the damn door.

When she answered, they were both half dressed. They claimed they had just taken a nap or some other bull shit.

I was so embarrassed. I could've beaten both their asses. But I have too much class for that, even back then. So I picked up what was left of my face and walked away.

Years later, when people asked my former girlfriend what happened; she would tell them I was just jealous because my man wanted her more. That used to piss me off, but I've forgiven her since she died in a car accident a few years back.

Needless to say, that was the last time I put all my love, trust, and time into a man. It's a viscous cycle. Some woman mistreats a man; he's then messed up for life, and treats women bad because he is fucked up. And round and round we go.

So, I've called it quits. I only worry about Lu Lu, and do what makes Lu Lu happy.

I must admit, it gets lonely at times, but I'll take the silence over a broken heart any day.

Deja

I don't know what I'm going to do. I haven't seen Derrick in over five years, and all the feelings just came flooding back. I would drop my panties right now if he asked me. Right here in the middle of the clubs grand opening.

I feel the same heat pulling us together that happened back at State.

Then he says, "Deja, I know your situation, and that he has hurt you, but that's still your husband."

"I know, but you need to let me worry about that. So, what are your plans for tonight, after the club?"

I can't believe the words that are falling out of my mouth!

"I have no plans. What's up? Are you sure you want to be seen with me? What do you have in mind Little Dee?"

"Let's get a room, just you and I. You know, so we can catch up."

"Girl, you are scaring me. I don't know about this Deja". His eyes were as big as saucers.

"Derrick, don't be nervous. I don't bite. Let me worry about my marriage. I just want to be with you tonight."
"Deja, it may not be a good thing to start this. You know how we are, or were. Once I start, I can't handle you taking it all away again". He looked so cute giving me those puppy dog eyes.

"Derrick, I can't promise you anything. I'm so lonely and confused. The one thing I do know is that I want to be with you tonight. Can you just give me that right now?"

"Okay. It's against my better judgment, but I need you tonight. After the club closes, I'll meet you at the back entrance. I'm driving a black Range Rover. Now you go be with your girls before they start suspecting shit. You know how they are."

He laughed that same laugh that used to make my hormones jump years ago. All I could do was smile and say, "okay". My panties were so wet; I stepped into the ladies room, took them off, and threw them away. They were no longer serving any type of purpose.

As I saw him walk across the club to his football buddies, I was thankful for running into him. Then I remembered my husband, our vows, and my faith. "What am I doing?" I whispered to myself.

Although I knew better, my mind was made up. For once I'm going to do what Deja wants to do, and not care. And tonight, Deja wants to do Derrick.

Gabby

This man is so fine. God has truly blessed him. If he licks his lips again, I'm liable to bite his fine ass. I've been abstinent for about six months now. This whole "down low brotha" thing has me a nervous wreck. Just my luck, I would get married, have kids, think I'm living the American dream, and then come home and catch my husband in bed with his best friend.

Just my luck.

But this LL Cool J lookin' brother has me straight re-thinking this abstinence thing.

He woke me out of my daydream when he started to speak, "Gabby, I have to run to the restroom, I'll be right back. Don't sneak out with some other brotha while I'm gone".

"You go ahead. I have some business to take care of. We'll hook back up in a minute".

I shook my head and smiled as he walked away. All I could muster up to say was "damn".

Why do these brothas make is so hard to do the Christian thing. I've been doing so well. The flesh is weak!

They say you usually know in the first 15 minutes of meeting someone if you are going to have sex with them. Hell, I knew in the first five that I wanted to drop my panties for this brotha. I need help, I've got chills just thinking about it.

Just my luck he'll have an itty bitty penis and I'll be regretting the fact that I broke my promise of abstinence to myself.

Just my luck.

Lu Lu

Look at this heffa, I'd know that stupid dazed look from a mile away. I know she's ready to hook up with Derrick. She really thinks she's fooling somebody walking around with stupid grin on her face. I'm about to burst her bubble.

"Hey Deja, what's up girl?" I mimicked the stupid smile she's wearing.

"Huh? Oh, hey Lu, you enjoying yourself sweetie?"

"Oh yeah, everything's cool. The club is packed; I really think it's going to be a success. The true test will be who comes back next weekend though."

"I've been ease dropping, and it seems everyone is really hyped about this new spot. You know Indy doesn't have a lot to do anyway".

"Yeah, so, enough about that. What's up with you and Derrick? You got that Mr. Carter daze in your eyes. What's up?" Yeah, she's busted.

"Girl nothing, it was just so good to see him. You know he plays for the Colts now."

"Girl please, I am not Gabby! Heffah I know you. What's up?"

"Okay, I knew I couldn't lie to you. Lu, I'm so lonely, and right now I really want to be with him. I'm not saying I want to end my marriage, but you know Derrick and I have this connection."

"You may not plan on ending your marriage, but your actions could very well end it Deja. Have you even considered David in all of this? I hope you know what you are getting your little self into."

I knew she would react this way; I don't need this shit right now. "Yes, I do know exactly what I'm getting into. You can talk to me all night; I'm not going to change my mind Lu".

"Hey, I'm not trying to change your mind. However, I am your girl, and I'm not going to lie to you. No matter what David has done in the past, don't look at me like that, I know David ain't perfect! Anyway, no matter what he has done, it doesn't make it right for you to cheat on him. You are a Christian, remember that!"

"Don't throw that in my face Lu Lu, you ain't perfect either. Fornication is just as much of a sin as adultery."

She's pissed at me, but I truly don't care. "I know that, I also know that I am a sinner, and I'm not trying to throw it in your face. As your sister it is my job to be honest with you, and we are not talking about me right now. I just hope you know what you are doing. And don't use my name in any lies to your husband because you know I am terrible at lying, and I personally don't want to lie to David".

"I know, I know. I apologize for my tone. That's why I love you because you are always honest. I wanna let you know, I'm going to get a room with Derrick tonight. Don't tell Gabby, she'll just freak out. I just wanted to let someone know where I would be."

"Deja, you need to think about this girl. This could potentially ruin your marriage".

"Lu Lu!"

"Okay, okay, don't give me that look. You're a grown ass women, and I'm gonna stay out of your grown ass business...but remember not to use my name in your cover up story". I rolled my eyes and walked away. Then I turned around and gave her a wink and a smile.

That's my girl, and although I had to tell her she was wrong. I know how she feels. I can empathize with her situation, but that doesn't make what she is doing right.

Poor thing.

Gabby

"Hey, what are you gals over here being all intense about?" I asked.

"Nothing girl, you know Lu Lu is crazy" Deja said as we smacked high fives on that one.

"Well, I need your strength. I'm about ready to rape this fine brother, Malcom. I'm getting weaker and weaker by the minute!" I confessed.

"Girl, I saw you dancing with that fine brotha! I can't help you with this one; my panties would have disintegrated when he walked up to me!" Lu Lu howled.

"I know that's right" Lu and Deja smacked high fives.

LuLu yawned, "Well ladies, the grand opening was a grand success! Group hug!"

"Well, I vote we let the staff worry about wrapping things up, and we get the heck up out of here." I said.
Lu Lu gave me a suspicious look. "What's your hurry Ms. Gabby? You leaving with LL's little brother or what? You ain't fooling nobody little missy. You're about ready to make a whore move aren't you?"

All I could do was smile, "I am not! We are headed out to breakfast. However, I am not responsible for what I might do to him after that!"

Deja yawned, "Okay, well, I will holla at you heffas tomorrow." She gives Lu Lu a wink.

I know something is up with Deja and Derrick. I know Lu knows, that must be the reason for that wink Deja just gave. I don't know why they think I am so sensitive. Maybe I am, but that doesn't make me stupid. I know how her and Derrick were, feelings like that are hard to shake.

"Okay, you ladies be careful! Smooches!" I said.

"Smooches!" all three of us yelled.

Deja

Just like he said, Derrick was waiting for me right outside the back entrance. I instantly got butterflies in my stomach.

I climbed up into the truck, and then I was confident again. I touched Derrick's upper thigh with great anticipation. I knew what lied ahead, and I couldn't wait. Although I love making love to my Husband, I always knew nobody every compared to sex with Derrick. There's this thickness to him that I've never seen in any other man. It's like our bodies were meant for one another. We fit together like a perfect puzzle. He also knew how to work it. He would begin like a slow passionate and seductive dance, and by the end he would be knocking that back out! I can't wait to feel him inside me.

"Deja! You can't start playing with him like that. Girl, I can't drive while he's hard, you gonna make us crash!" Derrick yelled.

"I'm sorry. I got caught up in the memories. I'll try to be good".

"Well, try no more, we're here." He smiled.

"Derrick! This is the Sybaris! You didn't need to spend all that money for one night."

"Actually, I booked it for the rest of the weekend. I was hoping you'd stay. Didn't you say your man was gone until the end of the month?"

"Yes, but let's see how tonight goes, then we'll think about the entire weekend".

Derrick began kissing me in that instant. The next thing I knew he swooped me up off my feet as if I was as light as a feather. Next, he gently laid me down on the bed. At that moment, I forgot about everything, my marriage, my problems, everything.

We made love at least three times before we fell asleep.

I awoke the next morning to Derrick looking down at me smiling while he stroked my hair.

"Hey beautiful. I see you still slobber in your sleep." He laughed.

"Shut-up, no I don't!"

"Yeah babe, you really do". He laughed as he handed me a tissue.

"Liar!" I yelled as I got up whipping my mouth while searching for my toothbrush. Derrick had already cleaned himself up and showered. I must have been in a coma.

I stepped out of the shower, and before I could even dry myself off, Derrick swooped me up and dumped me on the bed. He began kissing my breast ever so gently. At that point, my nipples were so hard they ached. He headed down to the center of my body, and I lost all control.

By the time his chocolate brown thickness entered my body, I felt like climbing the walls.

We went on in this manner until Sunday, we never left the room. Derrick ordered take out for all our meals, and he left one time to rent DVD's, but that was about it.

Most would think my husband would have been looking for me, but it's normal for him not to call at night. He called once Saturday evening, and Derrick went into the restroom to give me privacy, but all David wanted was to say hey and make sure the bills were paid. He never once asked where I was, or what I was doing. Probably because he was doing a little dipping of his own. Normally it would bother me, but right then I really didn't care.

"Well Little Dee, it's almost check out time. I think we should talk." Derrick said.

I finished with my hair and packed what little we had. Then I sat at the table to eat the food Derrick ordered from the Chinese restaurant.

"Babe, this weekend was wonderful! I missed you, and I never stopped loving you... I don't want this to end." He looked so sad.

"Derrick, I..."

"Wait, just let me finish. If you want me to go away and leave you alone, I will respect your choice. But, I know you are not happy in your marriage, and I want to be here for you."

"Derrick, I don't want to keep you mixed up in my confusion. You're a single man, and I want you to be happy."

"Deja, no other woman will make me happy. I've had several, and you know that, football groupies and more. But the only woman I've ever wanted is you."

"Derrick, I would love to be with you, but my situation is so messed up. I'm so confused right now; I don't know what to say."

"You don't have to say anything right now. All I'm asking is that you allow me to stay in your life while you sort things out."

"So you wanna be my secret lover?" I had to laugh.

"Exactly. I just want to be with you Dee. You're lonely, and I can help to fill that void".

"Derrick, I would love that, but how is that fair to you? I don't want you to get hurt."

"Let me worry about that".

"Okay, well, here's my cell number. That is how you can reach me."

"So", he smiled because he knew once again he had worn me down, "when can I see you again?"

"I don't know, you tell me".

"I'll pick you up for lunch tomorrow. What time do you have a break from teaching those bad ass kids?"

"11:00. I'll be thinking of you all day. And don't talk about my kids!" I smiled.

Derrick was just as sweet as I remembered, but I still know this relationship is wrong. But like the song says, I don't wanna be right.

Gabby

So, where do you wanna eat Ms. Gabby?" Malcolm said.

"Well it's late, we could do Denny's. They're open 24 hours. Can I trust going out with you in the middle of the night alone Mr. Malcolm?" I said with a tease, but I meant every word of it. I'd hate to be a story on the news tomorrow.

"Of course you can. I won't bite, that is unless you want me to." He grinned.

This man is most definitely trouble. I think my panties just fell off. I felt a tap on my shoulder that brought me back to reality. It was Lu Lu. Shit, what is she doing here?

"Hey girl, what is your crazy ass doing here?" Lu Lu yelled.

"Having an extra early breakfast with my new friend Malcolm. Malcolm, this is one of my best friends Lu Lu." They shook hands.

"Who are you here with Lu?" I looked around and saw no one.

"Vince". Just then Vince walked up behind her. Woo, now that man is fine, chocolate thunder fine! He and Lu Lu need to quite playing games and wasting time. They both swear they don't believe in relationships, but they do everything together. Go out together, sleep together, and take each other to family functions. Sounds like a steady relationship to me.

"Well," Lu said, "We're gonna leave you two to get acquainted. I'm too hungry to be polite". Lu Lu waived as they walked away.

"Well, now I have you all to myself Gabby. So now that I don't have to scream over the music, what's up with you? What's your story?" He smiled. Damn he is too fine.

"Hmmm. Well, nothing much, I'm 29 years old, I work at a law firm downtown, I'm a lawyer. No man, no kids. I'm a Christian woman, I attend East Side Baptist faithfully, I sing in the choir, and I teach Sunday School. So what's your story Malcolm?" I grinned.

"Well, you summed it up in a nut shell. Well, I work at Methodist hospital; I'm the head nurse on the Pediatric unit. No woman, no kids, I'm a Christian as well. I serve on the usher board, and last but not least, I've been abstinent for about a year."

Lord, you must be kidding!

"Really? I've been abstinent for about six months. I can certainly respect your commitment. It's been hard for me."

"Thank you Gabby. Most women either laugh, or don't believe me. Don't get me wrong I love women and love sex, but I prayed for the Lord to send me a good woman, and in order to readily receive my blessing, I feel that I need to stay committed to this, you know what I mean?" He said sincerely.

"I know exactly what you mean. It's not easy though. I must admit that."

"No it's not. I've taken plenty of cold showers to get me through." He laughed.

"Does that really work? Taking cold showers?" I asked.

"No, not really, but I'll try anything!" We both laughed.

The more this man talks, the more I'm attracted to him. I can most definitely see myself with him.

"Wait a minute; did you say you were a nurse on the pediatric unit at Methodist?"

"Yes." He grinned like he had something up his sleeve.

"I'm there once a week on my lunch breaks to read to the kids!" I said.

He grinned even harder, "I know, I've seen you come in there every Wednesday for the past few months. I just transferred a few months back from Los Angeles. My mom wasn't doing to well after my step-father passed away, so I thought it would be best if I moved here."

"So you've been watching me?"

"Yep, I've admired your dedication, and the glow in your eyes. I've admired the way the children respond to you. I had no idea you were a co-owner of the club though. When I walked in and saw the picture of you and your girls, I knew it was a sign. I knew at that moment that I had to get to know you." He grabbed my hand.

"You did huh?" I said attempting to play hard to get.

"Yes, I prayed to the Lord for a good woman, the right woman, and when I saw the picture, and then you, I took that as a sign."

"How can you be sure?" I asked.

"Come on now Gabby, you're a Christian. It's called faith right?"

"Yes, I do have faith. We'll see. I've been praying as well. We will just have to see what happens." I smiled.

"We will. So, when can I officially take you on a date?" He asked.

"You tell me."

"What are you doing Sunday?" He asked.

"Church, rest, and relaxation." I stretched my arms and yawned. "How about you come to church with me, I don't sing this Sunday. Then we can do lunch"

"Sounds perfect, I've heard a lot of good things about East Side Baptist. How about we do dinner instead of lunch. We could catch a movie after church, and then do dinner at Sullivan's. I really want to see that move "Ray"; they say Jamie Foxx should win an award for that one".

"That sounds wonderful. I've been wanting to see that movie as well. But if we go to Sullivan's you may want to make reservations. Just my luck we wouldn't be able to get a table."

"Gabby, I know you don't know me yet, but trust me, I got this." He laughed and released my hands as the waiter brought our food to the table.

"Okay", I laughed, "I apologize".

We ate and had wonderful conversations. This man is very intelligent. His conversation was so stimulating that I forgot all about the sexual tension I had earlier. Now that is surely a sign. A man that can stimulate my mind as well as my body. He is most definitely a keeper.

"Well, I'm about to fall asleep at this table. Although I hate to leave." I yawned.

"Well, Gabby, we have plenty of time to get to know one another. I'm going to pay the tab; I'll meet you out at the car."

I stood at the car and waited for Malcolm. This has turned out to be a very pleasant experience.

"Are you ready beautiful?"

"Yes, I'm ready handsome."

"Okay, now where do you live?"

We talked so much on the way home, it seemed like the ride was five minutes long. Although I know it was at least 30 minutes.

"Here we are" He yawned. His eyes were red, and I knew he was very tired.

"Malcolm, I was thinking. Instead of spending money on Sullivan's Sunday, we could go to church, then the movie, and I could cook dinner here at my house."

"I'd love that. So you mean to tell me, a fine sistah like you, slammin' body, successful career, seems to have a beautiful personality, can cook too? I must be dreaming!" He smiled.

"See," I said, "You never judge a book by its cover". I laughed.

"Touché."

Well, Mr. Malcolm, I'm going to have to bid you a good night before I fall flat on my face. I am exhausted!"

He then leaned over and kissed me slowly on my cheek. His lips were so soft I melted. I must be dreaming. But if I am, Lord don't let me wake up.

I sashayed up to my front door because I knew he was watching. I may have to try one of those cold showers right about now. I can't wait until Sunday!

Deja

This past weekend with Derrick was amazing. He took me to lunch during my prep yesterday, and I didn't want to leave him. I may be in trouble, there's no may be to it, I am in trouble. I've always loved this man. I've always kicked myself for not ever giving him the opportunity to be with me. I just knew it would have been bad.

I'm so confused. I haven't heard from David since Saturday. It's that type of shit that I'm talking about. I called him last night, and he rushed me off the phone. I know I heard a woman's voice in the background, but he'll never admit it. He acts like I'm crazy, but I know him.

He'll come home, and act like we have the best thing since sliced bread going on, and then he'll leave again, and treat me like shit. Lord, what am I supposed to do? I feel like I'm about to explode, and the only thing that keeps me sane is Derrick.

What? Who the hell is calling my house at this hour, it's eleven o'clock at night. "Hello", I said in an angry tone. I hate when people call anonymous. But at this hour, I'm answering so I can cuss someone clean out.

"Hello, may I speak with Deja?" the woman's voice said.

"Speaking, who is this?"

"Look, I hate to bother you, but my name is Sandy. I want to apologize and inform you at the same time".

"What? Who is this? What are you talking about?"

"I met your husband, David, about a year ago at a business convention in Los Angeles. I didn't know he was married, until about a month ago. We've been dating all this time."

"You're kidding right? I'm supposed to be receptive to a total stranger calling me in the middle of the night to tell me she's been sleeping with my husband? Is this a joke?"
"Look Deja, I don't blame you for being upset, but your husband has been playing both of us. He's met my family; he's even met my 8 year old son. He's taken him to ball games and everything. Do you have e-mail? If so, I'll send you the pictures right now."

"Yes, I have e-mail. Just send it to deja@divas.com. I apologize for my attitude; I'm just trying to sort out what you're telling me."

"Trust me, I understand. I was furious. I promise you I did not know he was married. He had no ring, and I had no reason not to believe him. Then he called me Deja when he was here a couple of weeks ago. When I asked him who Deja was, he brushed me off like I was crazy, so I let it go. But something told me there was more."

"Well, how did you find out?"

"Before he left for Korea, he left his wallet here in a pair of jeans he asked me to send to the cleaners. When I opened it, there was a picture of you plain as day. On the back it said "David and Deja Honeymoon". I haven't confronted him yet, but I decided to find you. I called information in Indianapolis because I knew his company was headquartered there. It was just that simple."

"I see."

"Deja, I just thought you should know. There's no reason for you to be in the dark. Did you get the e-mail?"

"Yes, I just opened it." I clicked on the e-mail from this woman calling me in the middle of the night. There stood my David, my husband with this 8 year old stranger. He looked so happy. I instantly got pissed. He's taking this woman's son around like the child he never had, but told me he was too young, and it was too early in his career to have children. My heart dropped about ten inches, and I began to feel sick.

"Look, what's your name, Sandy?" I asked, "I appreciate your 'woman to woman' call, but this is my husband. There's a huge difference between husband and boyfriend. Like I said, I appreciate you calling, but I need to let you go." I said.

"I totally understand the way you feel Deja. I love David. I thought the Lord sent this man to my son and I, and he told me he wanted to marry me..."

"Stop, look Sandy, you can have him". I hung up the phone. I couldn't take anymore.

I paced the floors, I walked around. I looked at my house, and thought about the last five years. I immediately felt as though I've wasted valuable time. I've wasted five years of my life on a lie. I then became enraged. I want to kill him! How could he do this to me!

I went to my bedroom, where I lay in the fetal position and cried all night.

The next morning I had to call into work. I've never called in, so I have plenty of sick days. I informed them that I had the flu and wouldn't be in the rest of the week. I feel like I'm dying. I'm so confused I don't know what to do. My damn phone has been ringing off the hook, and my cell has been blowing up as well.

Now who in the hell is knocking on my door. Shit, it's Lu and Gabby; I forgot I was supposed to go to lunch with them. I guess I have to go ahead and open the door.

"Hey girl" Lu Lu yelled, "You look like shit, what is up with you? You never call into work, and you didn't tell us we wouldn't be doing lunch today."

"I know Deja, you could have at least called someone", Gabby co-signed as she closed the front door.

Lu Lu looked at me and tilted her head, "You've been crying, what's going on?"

I could barely speak. I felt so weak; I didn't have the energy to even tell the story. I just handed them the pictures of David with his mistress' son.

"What the fuck? Is this his son? What in the hell?" Lu Lu yelled. Her mouth is so fowl.

Gabby just sat there dumb founded.

"No," I said, "It's not his son; it's his girlfriend's son. He's been dating her for about a year, and she called me last night to let me know. She had no idea he was married. She found a picture of me in his wallet. Our honeymoon picture or something. So then the bitch played detective and found our home number.

"Deja," Gabby said, "You shouldn't be upset with her, he played both of you"

"Right," Lu said, "You need to fly her ass here on the same day David is due back, and bust his ass out, that's what I would do".

"No, I can't wait two more weeks, I need to call him now." I immediately picked up the phone and dialed his hotel.

"Hello?" A woman answered with a heavy Korean accent.

"Yes, may I speak to David?" I asked about to come through the phone and commit homicide.

"Hold on please". She said.

"Lu and Gabby, a woman just answered his hotel phone. I think I'm about to faint".

Next I heard my husband's voice in the back ground. "Lee, didn't I tell you never to answer my phone!" He yelled at her in a voice I'd never heard him use. Then the phone hung up.

I immediately dialed his room back.

"Hello?" He answered in the loving tone I'm accustomed to.

"David, who is Lee?" I asked.

"Lee, I don't know, who is that babe?" He asked.

No this nigga is not gonna sit here and act brand new on me. I can't believe this shit.

"David, I just called, and your girlfriend answered the phone. Don't sit there and act like I'm crazy. Please." I begged.

"Deja, don't start tripping." He sighed.

"Well. We will talk about Lee later; right now I'm concerned with Sandy." I yelled.

"Baby, let's talk about this when I get home. I really can't talk right now".

"No, I want to talk about it right now!"

"Deja, you know I love you, please let's talk about this when I get back. Please babe, I'm begging" He cried.

I hung up the phone. I don't believe this shit. He must have lost his damn mind. And I must be dumber then a box of rocks. I began to feel sick, my mouth got salty, and I ran to the bathroom and puked my guts out. Lu Lu and Gabby really need to leave me alone in my embarrassment. I just want to be left alone. But I know they won't leave.

Who is Lu Lu talking too? "Here Deja, it's Derrick. I tried to get him off the phone, but he won't hang up. He said you stood him up yesterday and he's worried.

I reluctantly took the phone from Lu. "Hello?" I know I sound like a hot mess.

"Dee, what's wrong? You sound terrible. What happened yesterday?"

I began to cry. I could barely speak, "I just ....."

"I'm outside your house. I knew something was wrong, I felt it. Open the door Deja."

"No, you don't have to come in, I'll be..." He cut me off. "Open the damn door Deja". He said in a stern tone.

Lu Lu, please go open the door for Derrick.

"Are you sure you want to do that?" She looked confused.

"Yes, you know he will stand there all day if you don't let him in, just open the damn door! I actually want all of you to leave, but I know you won't, so one more unwanted guest won't make a difference will it?" I yelled. I hate to yell at my girl like that, but I had to yell at someone.

"Look Deja, I'm going to let you get away with talking to me like that this time, but don't push it sweet heart!" She yelled back.

"What the hell is going on up in here? Why is Deja crying"? He pleaded with Lu Lu.

"Calm down man, she's in her room, follow me. I'll forewarn you, she is in a fowl mood." Lu Lu said.

"Deja, what's wrong. You look like you've been crying all night!" I could tell he was very worried. I threw the pictures his way.

He looked at them and laughed while shaking his head. "This doesn't shock me at all. I told you he was a player Dee". He wanted to take those words back as I began to cry.

He slipped his shoes off and lay in the bed behind me. He rocked and held me, and I felt so safe in that moment.

After sometime, I fell asleep. When I woke up, I heard laughing and talking, and I smelled chicken frying. I walked out of the bedroom, and saw Gabby, Lu Lu, and Derrick in the kitchen cooking up a storm laughing and talking. I immediately began to cry.

Derrick ran over to me. "What's wrong babe, do you wanna go back to bed?"

"No, I'm crying because you guys are still here, I thought you left. You're cooking and cleaning." I cried harder.

"Well, what's the problem"? Lu Lu and Gabby walked over.

"Nothing, it's just a blessing to have people in your life that love you as much as you love me" We all stood in a circle and embraced.

It felt like we were at State all over again. Derrick and my girls together, we had a ball. We stayed up all night. We laughed, talked, reminisced, played spades. I didn't have a chance to even think about David.

At about 3am, I fixed up the spare bedroom for my girls. We had all had a little too much to drink to consider driving home. Not to mention none of us drink anyway.

Derrick started to slip his shoes on. "Where are you going?" I asked.

"I didn't think you'd want me to stay, and you know I don't drink, so I'll be fine". He is so sweet.

"No, please stay. I just want you to hold me tonight. I need you Derrick." I begged.

"You don't have to ask me twice!" He slid off his shoes and hung up his coat. "Are you sure about this? I know you're going through things right now, but this is still David's home. I feel like I'm crossing the line." I put my hand over his mouth to stop him from speaking. I didn't want to think, I just wanted to go back to bed, and I wanted him with me.

Gabby

I can't believe what is going on with Deja and David. It's so heart breaking. I couldn't even tell them about Malcolm because it seemed like it would be in bad taste to tell them how happy I was while she felt so bad.

It's so sweet of Derrick to stay there with her; at least we don't have to worry about her doing something crazy. I always thought they were soul mates. It kind of shocked me when she fell for David, he's nothing like Derrick. I guess I always assumed they would be together. Although, Dr. Phil said if a person leaves their spouse for their soul mate, the relationship is doomed from the start. I mean, hopefully he is wrong, but he is an expert.

Anyway, Malcolm and I had a wonderful time at church last Sunday. I'm going to visit his church next. I wound up having to work from home that evening, and instead of cooking for him, he came over and cooked for me. I was very impressed. He pampered me royally. He cooked, served chilled champaign, and the whole nine. He messaged my feet and my neck, I was in seventh heaven.

I'm making up for it tonight. I'm going to his condo to fix him dinner and return the favor. He made Italian at my house, so tonight I'm cooking soul food. I made the greens yesterday, they're always better the 2nd day. I'm going to fry chicken, yams, mac and cheese. I'm going to get this brotha good and full today.

I get butterflies in my stomach just thinking about seeing him tonight. He lives on the northwest side of town, so I'm on the highway right now. The Fantasia CD is the bomb. I rooted for her all last year on American Idol. I am truly an Idol junky. I never voted in previous seasons, but Fantasia had me hitting redial on my cell phone like a true fanatic. I knew she would win. She is original, and that is what most people want.

I'm listening to "Truth Is" right now. This child truly has talent, and to be so young.

Malcolm's place is really nice. You can tell a man lives here alone though. I think I will by him some art for these bare walls. The condo has a lot of potential, but he's only been here a few months though.

I knocked on the door with anticipation. "Hello, may I help you?" an older woman answers the door.

"Hi, I'm looking for Malcolm" I said questionably.

"Hello, you must be Gabriel, come on in baby". She smiled "I'm Connie, Malcolm's mom. He told me you were coming over today, and I stayed a little longer. I just wanted to be nosey and see what had him so bubbly lately. I hope you don't mind". Her smile was so genuine.

"No ma'am. I don't mind at all. It's very nice to meet you, I've heard so much about you already." I shook her hand, and she stretched out her arms and gave me a hug instead.

"I'm going to get ready to leave, but I just had to meet you. Malcolm has been prayerful and patient waiting for the right woman to come into his life, and I think it has been worth the wait". She said.

"I hope so Connie, but we've only been dating a couple of weeks". I smiled.

"Yes honey, but when God brings two people together, it doesn't take long to figure it out. Now I have to go before Malcolm has a heart attack". She gave me another hug.

"Mom, you aren't out here scaring Gabby to death are you?" Malcolm kissed my forehead.

"No, we were just having a little girl talk". I said and then winked my eye at Connie. She's a beautiful woman. Malcolm is thirty-three years old, and he told me she is fifty-three. This woman doesn't look old enough to have a child twenty-three, let alone thirty-three. I'd pay big bucks to look like her at fifty-three. The woman is bad, not a wrinkle or a gray hair in sight. She also can't be more than a size 8. She's just beautiful. She looks a lot like Diane Carol.

"We'll catch up more Gabriel. Maybe we could do lunch or something. I work at the Bank One building downtown, close to your law firm. I'd really like that." She glowed.

"Sure, I would like that too." I handed her my card, and she did the same. "Let's try and get together this week." I said.

"Okay dear, see you soon" she said patting my shoulder. "And I better see you soon as well", she said grabbing Malcolm chin and turning it towards her. She kissed him on the cheek, and off she went.

"Well, I hope that wasn't too uncomfortable. She did that on purpose, she wanted to meet you since I've been talking about you so much."

"No, it wasn't uncomfortable at all. She seems really nice. What does she do at the Bank One building?" I asked.

"She works in Human Resources. She's been there for years. Each year she says she going to retire, but every time someone whines about her leaving, she decides to stay. She has a big heart." He said, glowing as he talked about his mother.

They say if a man knows how to treat his mother, then he'll know how to treat his woman. I hope that's a true statement.

"So, are you ready for dinner dear?" I asked.

"Sure am. The Pacers are about to play, do you mind if we watch the game while you cook?" He asked.

"Nope, I was hoping you'd say that because I don't want to miss the game. Not after the brawl in Detroit, I hope the Pacers mop the floor with the Piston's. They really pissed me off suspending all of our players."

"I know, pissed me off too, I didn't know you were a b-ball fan." He smiled.

"Love it!" I yelled. "I love basketball. You may have to bear with me during football season, but give me an NBA game any day."

"My kind of woman", he said as he kissed my lips. That was the first time he kissed me on the lips. I got so weak in the knees I almost dropped the groceries. But brotha is so smooth; he had already grabbed the bottom of the groceries to carry them over to the table.

Meanwhile, I'm standing there like I'm in shock. Oh shit, I think my panties just fell off!

"Do you need any help Gabby?" He asked, breaking my trance. "I'm not good with fried chicken, for some reason mine never turns out right, but I can help with the sides."

"No, I'll be fine. I didn't get a chance to help you, so I'll do the cooking tonight Malcolm." I said.

"That's because you were working on that case. I have no work to do, so I'm going to help. It's either that or pace

around behind you like a bored puppy. Your choice." He laughed.

"Okay, then you need to help me." I laughed. As I started to unload the groceries, I felt his arms come around my waist from behind. My hormones began to jump. He kissed the back of my neck and then turned me around and began to kiss me. His lips were so soft I thought I was going to melt.

I tried to pull away, but he pulled me back. Then he tried to pull away, but I pulled him back. Then instantly, we both pulled away. "Gabby, I am so sorry! I just couldn't help myself." He looked scared.

"There's no need to apologize Malcolm. I couldn't help myself either. It's really hard trying to do the right thing, I mean REALLY hard." I fanned myself.

"I know, but I really do believe the Lord brought you into my life, so we have to try and be strong".

"I know Malcolm, but you are going to have to help me because a sistah is weak!" We both laughed and began cooking dinner.

"Hey, you remember I told you about my girl Deja right?" I asked.

"Yeah, is she okay? I know this has to be hard for her, my heart would be crushed". He replied.

"Yeah, she's okay. She's been staying at Derrick's place which is about five minutes from here. We should take them a plate".

"That's cool with me, maybe we could play a game of spades or something while we're watching the game." He said.

See, I knew I liked this man. Most men wouldn't be concerned about a women's girlfriend. They wouldn't give a damn, and if they did decide to go over there with me, they wouldn't want to stay.

"Okay, I got the food together, let's go". I said putting on my coat. I think we would have agreed to do anything to get out of that house. One more minute alone, and we would have been butt naked on the kitchen floor.

"Who is it?" I heard Deja yell through the door.

"Who it is!" I yelled back.

"You are a crazy heffah, you know that right?" She laughed, "My my, who is this?" She asked.

"This is my friend Malcolm. Malcolm, this is Deja, my girl". I introduced.

"Hello Deja, nice to finally meet you. I've heard a lot about you" Malcolm shook her hand.

"Well, I'm sorry I haven't heard enough about you yet." She took Malcolm's hand and pulled him into the house and towards the kitchen to put away the food. That fool left me standing at the front door. She is crazy. I hope Malcolm is prepared for Deja's 20 questions.

"Hey Ms. Gabby!" I heard Derrick yell coming down the hall. "What's up home girl?"

"Nada homie, what's up with you?" I said in a playful tone. "Thank you so much for taking care of our girl, you are a true sweetie!" I gave him a hug.

"Gabby, I wouldn't have it any other way. David is an asshole, and I saw this coming from a mile away. But she's in good hands now."

All I could do was smile. He always had loved Deja, she just couldn't see it.

"So home slice, what did you and your new boyfriend bring us to grub on" Derrick asked.

I knew he was going to attempt to embarrass me in front of Malcolm, but Malcolm seemed to get a kick out of it, so I let it slide.

"We cooked some soul food. We got a little bit of everything, so let's eat. I'm starving!" I yelled.

"So Mr. Malcolm. What are you're intentions with my sistah here?" Deja smiled.

"Well, I think God sent her to me, so I'm just biding my time and trying to get to know her better. She's beautiful, intelligent, God fearing, and beautiful...Oh I already said that didn't I" he laughed.

"Okay, you guys are making me blush, stop it!" I said.

"Gabby, have you talked to Lu Lu. I think she is with Vince. We should call them up." Deja said.

The next thing you know, Lu and Vince were walking in the door. I never laughed so hard in one night in all of my life. I laughed so hard my sides split. The men put on a dance contest, and not one of them could actually dance. We played cards, we bumped some old school 70's music and danced, we told old college stories to Malcolm and Vince, we had a wonderful time.

It was the first time in years that I could remember the three of us having men that all got along. I've missed this. And I know it was good for Deja. She looked like her old self again.

Lu Lu

We had so much fun over Derrick's house the other night, I could still sit here and laugh picturing Vince, Derrick, and Malcolm attempting to dance. They are some fine brotha's, but dancing is not their forte. That night was hilarious.

It just dawned on me, that whenever I have fun with a man, it's always with Vince. I've grown so used to him. We do everything together, but we have no label. We are just friends. I love him, I really do, but I'm afraid if I put the "boyfriend" label on him things will fall apart. I'm not quite sure why that happens, it just does.

I've met all of his family; his mother is convinced we are getting married, no matter what we tell her. She's so sweet. And my mother thinks Vince is my last hope at a husband and children.

It's gotten to the point where I lie awake at night thinking about him. He is my chocolate thunder. I want to call him all the time, but I don't want to come off like I'm sprung or something. We go for days without talking because we each have to see who will break and call first. I know it sounds so stupid, but it's a vulnerability issue. Neither of us wants to appear that way, but truth is, we both are. It's sad to be in this position. We could both miss out on a wonderful relationship. However, neither of us believes in relationships. Isn't that uncanny?

Was that a knock at my door? "Who is it?" I yelled out.

"Who it is!" the voice yelled back. It was Vince's crazy self. I know he picked that line up from one of my girlfriends. He's been around them entirely too much.

"I opened the door". How is it that he always pops up when I'm thinking about him, too weird?

"Hey Lu, I was thinking about you, and I needed you, so I came over. I hope that's okay, I was playing ball right around the corner".

"No baby, you know it's cool. You're the only one that can come over here without calling first".

"Do you mind if I hop in the shower?" He asked as he walked to the bathroom without an answer. I didn't even bother to answer because he was already in the bathroom with the water running.

At that moment, I jumped up and went and put on matching underwear from Victoria's Secret. I couldn't let him see me in the Wonder Woman boy shorts I had on, they are just for lounging around the house.

When Vince came out of the shower, I had candles lit, and I had the old Carl Thomas CD playing. The track "Lady Lay Your Body" was playing. Each time I listen to that song I think of Vince. He doesn't know that though. There's a phrase in the beginning of the song, "Last night I think I fell in love with you, it was from a window watching you around my way. I was to shy to even call to you, so I wrote these words to make it easier to say". That verse sends chills down my spine.

That's when he came out of the bathroom, butt naked and dripping. I was so shocked, I spit out the Pepsi I was drinking. I didn't know what to say. I mean, Vince and I have sex all the time, but we never involved romance. It was always a last minute, I was about to go home, but I couldn't help it type thing.

Then he walked over to me, and I had to hold my breath. He bent down on his knees so that we were eye to eye while I sat on the couch. He began to undress me. It was slow and sensual at first. I thought that was sweet, but he knows I'm a rough rider type of girl. He must have sensed it because he damn near tore my panties off. He began to rub my clit with his middle finger slowly, then fast. I felt like I was about to lose complete control of myself. I taught him months ago how to give a woman a quick orgasm.

Right before I reached my peak, he stopped. I wanted to scream! He was teasing me, and my body was yearning for him. He got up and walked away.

"Are you trying to be funny?" I asked not amused.

"Had to get my raincoat baby." He answered.

Within seconds, he was back. When he inserted himself inside me, I almost lost my breath. See, this brotha is very well endowed. I've had longer, but length is nothing without width. And Vince had both. Our bodies fit together like pieces to a puzzle. He knew just how to fulfill me. I of course know how to please him.

When we were finished, I jumped up to fulfill our hot wash cloth ritual. We gotta keep it clean. Some may enjoy lying around in the juices, but not I.

"Lu, we need to talk." Vince said as I walked away.

"Talk to me baby, I'm listening." I said from the bathroom. I didn't like the sound of this at all. Whenever somebody says that, trouble is near.

"Lu Lu, you can either hear me out, or ask me to leave..."

"Why would I..." He put a finger up to my mouth. He knows me well. Once I get started, it's hard to shut me up.

"I know our little shared philosophy on relationships, but I have to admit to you that I was wrong. We've been kickin' it, or whatever it is that we've been doing for quite sometime now." He took a breath.

"Two years!" I blurted out.

"Yes, two years. I love you Lu Lu. I have for sometime now. I'm not asking you to marry me; I'm just asking that we try having a normal relationship. You know, no other women, no other men, just you and I." His eyes were pleading with mine.

"Vince, you know I love you. But from experience I know putting labels on things doesn't work. I've tried it. I've been down that road before. Been there, done that, told the story, and wrote a book about it. I value our friendship, and I don't want to lose you."

He grabbed my face and kissed me ever so gently. "Lu Lu, I've been there before as well, but I can't continue this way. This lifestyle may work for you, but it doesn't work for me anymore. It's not enough."

"So what are you saying Vince?" I asked already knowing the answer.

"I'm saying I love you, and I want a commitment. But you don't. Is that correct?" He asked.

"No, I don't." I admitted. I am so hardheaded sometimes.

"Well Lu, as much as I love you, I'm afraid I'm going to have to let you go." He said as he got up and started to dress himself.

"Well, I can understand that." I said half heartedly. I was actually heart broken.

"Okay, well, I'll see you around Lu." He said. He seemed so sad.

I love Vincent, I really do, but I can't allow myself to be crushed again. I guess it is just meant for me to be alone. I'm going to miss Vince. I've grown attached to him.

Did I just mess up?

Yep, I believe I did...

Deja

I've truly been blessed with a good group of people in my life. My "extended" family. Derrick, Lu Lu, and Gabby. If it weren't for them, I wouldn't have made it through the night after Sandy called. Especially after I called David and that Korean heffah answered the phone.

Well, today is the day that David comes home. As a matter of fact he should be walking through the door any minute. Derrick made it a lot easier to make it through the two weeks. He is so thoughtful. He didn't try to make love to me not once. And I stayed at his house. As a matter of fact, we haven't made love since the weekend at the Sybaris. He's so patient and understanding, I really don't understand it. He says it's because he truly loves me. Maybe I don't understand what love truly is.

"Deja!" David yelled as he fumbled through the front door with all of his luggage.

"Deja, are you here baby?" He yelled again.

"I'm here David, please stop yelling" I said calmly.

"Oh hey baby", he tried to kiss me as I jerked away.

"Come on now Deja. I can explain everything that's been going on." He said.

"So, who's filing for a divorce? Should I, or will you take care of it. You make the most money, I think that is only fair" I said coldly.

"Divorce? Wait a minute, we haven't even discussed this yet babe. Come on now. We can't throw five years away off of one bitch's phone call." He pleaded.

"Yes, off one bitch's phone calls, the pictures of you and her child, the Korean bitch in your hotel room, and all of your damn lies." I began to raise my voice, and then I thought about what Derrick said about staying calm so that I can focus. I took a deep breath and stepped back.

"Deja, I know I messed up. But I promise you baby I don't want anybody else but you. I will do anything, anything. I cursed that bitch out for calling the house and..." I stopped him mid sentence by putting up my hand.

"David. Save it. You had no right to curse her out. She didn't do anything wrong. You dated this woman for an entire year. You became a part of her sons' life. You made her think she'd found a man, a man to be her husband and to help raise her son. You misled her, so why is she a bitch all of a sudden".

He looked down and began to cry. But for the first time in five years of marriage, I did not feel sorry for him at all. He just looked pitiful.

"Deja, you know I love you. It's just hard being away from you so much. I was thinking with my dick, and not my head, baby you don't understand." He cried.

"David, just stop. Don't act new with me. That thinking with my dick statement is a crock of shit. You use that line every time you get caught up. I'm tired of it. You do not respect me as your wife. All the time you were spending with her, you could have been home spending with me. But, now it is too late. I've already moved all my things into a condo. A girl can do a lot in two weeks. I bought a condo on the other side of town. Thank you for keeping my credit perfect." I said as I grabbed my purse, keys, and my last rolling suit case.

"Wait, you've already moved out?" He said angrily.

"Yep, I moved yesterday. Don't worry, we had two of everything. I'm not one of those bitter and vindictive women that would clean you out. I took one set of furniture, one computer, one of everything. So, you can feel free to move Sandy and her son here". I said as I walked away ever so calmly. I actually felt relieved, like jogging.

"Deja, wait!" He ran out behind me. "If you leave, don't try and come back!" He yelled.

Was that supposed to be a threat? I turned around slowly and laughed, "David, don't flatter yourself". I turned back around and walked to my truck.

Gabby

"Malcolm, I really enjoyed your church today. The choir got off! I remember them from the Baptist convention." I said.

He smiled. "I'm glad you came. I know you noticed all the frowns and scowls coming your way. Sorry about that".

"Of course, how could I not. That type of stuff doesn't bother me though. It's kind of interesting. Jealousy is a motha sucka. I guess I have what they all want huh?" I laughed.

"Yes, it's a shame how women at church behave. Sometimes they are worse then women in the club".

"Well, when a woman sees a nice looking successful man, not to mention a Christian man, that is husband territory. That's when they try and sink there claws in." I said.

"My mom thinks it's because I haven't dated anyone in the church, and curiosity kills the cat. They want to know what the secret is. This one sistah, I'll have to point her out to you next time. She said I must be gay or a DL brotha since I didn't talk to her. She even started spreading rumors around the church!" He laughed. "Desperado is her new name!"

"That's a shame. Well, I guess I will be hated then huh?" I smiled.

"You got it. Don't worry though Ma has your back. She knows how to kindly put folks in their place. And most of the women there really respect her." He said as he kissed my face.

Things are going really well, but it is getting harder and harder not to rape this man. We spend so much time together. I just don't know how I am going to keep this up. My feelings are confusing me as well. I don't think I've ever actually been in love, so I'm not quite sure what it feels like. But I feel that I love Malcolm. It must be lust or infatuation, but I know I feel something. It has nothing to do with sex because I'm not getting any; he stimulates me on so many levels. I don't know what it is. I've prayed on it, I've even talked to my pastor about it. He said he only knew his wife for two months before he proposed, and they've been married for 25 years.

I'm not saying I'm ready to marry Malcolm, but I am saying I do believe I am in love.

"Gabby" he said as he broke my train of thought. "I've been thinking, we've been spending practically everyday together since the opening of the club. And I prayed for you, I know you are the one because God told me in so many ways. I just want to let you know that I do love you, and I am committed to getting to know you in a committed relationship. I can understand if this is too sudden for you, but I ask that you pray on it because I am sure". He said as he pulled up to a red stop light and looked over at me.

"Lord, what am I supposed to say?" I silently prayed. And then the Lord gave me a sense of reassurance.

"Malcolm, I understand how you feel. I've never felt this way so suddenly about anyone. I do believe the Lord brought you into my life, and I do believe I love you too." I looked him straight in the eye for the first time.

We suddenly began to kiss until the car behind us began to blow his horn violently. We both jumped as if we had forgotten we were in the car. "You better drive before he gets road rage and gets out of his car", I said as we both laughed.

Deja

As I pulled up to my new condo. I felt a sense of relief and independence. It felt wonderful! The condo was ten minutes from the school I taught in, and fifteen minutes away from the club. "Home sweet home!" I yelled as I fell down on the bed. Then I heard knocking at the door.

"Who is it?" I yelled through the door. I'm too short to look through the peephole.

"It's me Little Dee." Derrick said.

I opened the door and smiled. It was so good to see him. I'd gotten so used to waking up with him.

"Hey babe, are you alright?" He asked. "I know dick head came home today. Did you remain calm? No use giving him any of your energy, save it for your kids at the school."

"I'm fine, he tried to take me there, but I didn't let him. He told me if I left to never come back. I thought that was funny." I laughed.

"Well, he's just grasping at straws to make you stay. He doesn't realize what he has done has made you stronger, not weaker. Brotha's like that crack me up" he laughed.

We hugged, but we were interrupted by banging at the door. Who ever it was, he was banging violently like the police. Derrick walked towards the door. He was definitely tall enough to look through the peephole.

"It's David". He said as he looked back at me. "Do you want me to leave or stay?" He asked.

"I want you to stay, he no longer has a say in my life choices". I said as I opened the door.

Out of respect Derrick stepped into the next room. David came barging through the door.

Malcolm

I can't wait for Gabby to meet the rest of my family. I know they will love her just as much as I do.

All of a sudden my moms decided to throw a BBQ for the immediate family. I know it's just her way of letting her nosy ass sisters meet Gabby. I tell you, that woman can not hold water. As soon as she left my house, she went straight to them with the 411 about Gabby. At least it was all good info though.

I told Gabby she was the guest of honor, and surprisingly she was excited about meeting my family. So I guess it is all good.

"Who is it?" I yelled after hearing a light knock on the door. I knew what response I would get if it was Gabby.

"Who it is!" She yelled back as country as ever. This girl just tickles me. She is crazy.

I opened the door and greeted my girl with a kiss on the lips. Her lips are so soft; I just wanted to lay her down right there in the middle of my moms living room floor. She makes a brotha weak. "Lord, please give me strength. You know I'm trying", I prayed silently.

"Hey sweetie, you okay?" Gabby asked. She has know idea.

"Yeah babe, I'm cool. You ready to meet the fam?" I asked while poking her in the side.

"Ready!" She smiled.

"I'll have to forewarn you, the women are cool, but the uncles are off the hook. I mean embarrassingly off the hook. As fine as you are, they will try and eat you up." I looked at her seriously.

"Don't worry Malcolm, I got this. I can handle it. I got some crazy relatives myself". She smiled coolly.

And then it happened. Five minutes after Gabby stepped into the room and I introduced her. Uncle Clyde yelled out, "Carmel Delight! Damn girl, it's been years, but you still look good!" Then he went into a long drawn out story of how Gabby could shake it like no other over at Pure Passion. It's a local strip club from back in the day.

I looked at Gabby, and for the first time I saw her shaken. She turned as red as a damn beet, and then she turned and walked away. She kissed my mother and headed out of the door.

I ran out behind her, but she never slowed down. "Gabby wait!" I yelled.

"Malcolm, I can't right now." She said. Her voice was quivering, and she began to cry. "I'm so embarrassed".

Before I could get to her car, she rolled out. I can't believe this shit. "God would you send me a stripper", I said to myself. I really thought Gabby was a gift from God, but would he send me a woman capable of such things? I remember the story about Jezebel, but I am totally confused now.

Maybe Gabby wasn't what I thought. I guess it is better to end it now than drag it on.
My heart tells me yes, but my mind tells me to run like hell!

David

I can't believe I fucked up like this. I don't think this one is repairable. I never actually thought I would lose Deja. Not over Sandy, Lee, or any other woman. Deja is the dream wife. I just get lonely being on the road so much, and my hormones have a mind of their own. I mean damn, sometimes I'm gone for 3, 4 weeks at a time. That's a long time to go with no bootie. But that's no excuse. I had no reason to put Deja through all of this, she deserves better, she's a good girl. Lord, please tell me what to do!

It was almost a year ago when I met Sandy. I knew I was in trouble when I first laid eyes on her. This woman had a body that made my dick throb instantly. I tried my best to stay away from her, but she wound up on my project team for the entire conference. What are the odds of that? It's the devil, that's what it is.

Next thing I knew, we were back at her place. That bitch is a liar too. She told Deja she didn't know I was married. I had on my wedding ring shining as bright as day. She asked me, and I told the truth. I even showed her a picture. She said she wasn't tripping.

I do a lot of traveling to Los Angeles, which is where she lives. She said she was cool with everything; I would be hers when I'm in LA. I should have known she was crazy.

I saw the pictures she e-mailed Deja. She told her it was a picture of me with her damn son. That bitch doesn't even have kids, at least not that I know of. That was a picture of me with one of the kids the corporation sponsors. We have a mentoring program for African American boys, and I took a picture with Dante, he's one of my favorites. Sandy thought it was so cute, she kept it.

I can't believe I got myself into this mess! I've got to tell Deja the truth. Even if she leaves me, I don't want her to think I was playing daddy to some other woman's child. Especially when I told her we need to wait to make our own. Lord, please help me.

Vince

I was totally caught off guard when Lu Lu said she didn't want a relationship. That girl is ice cold. She's like a dude I'm telling you. As a matter of fact, messing with her is like looking in a mirror at myself. She is exactly what I used to be. I can't take it.

Who the heck is calling me, I'm really not in the mood to be bothered today.

"Hello?" I said angrily.

"Hey stranger! You can't return nobody's phone calls huh?"

"Who is this?" I asked.

"Dang, you used to be my homie now you act like you don't know me!" she laughed, "This is Kenda, you forgot me already?"

"No baby, it's just been a while. I didn't catch your voice." I lied.

I actually had forgotten all about her. I guess Lu Lu had my nose open so wide I couldn't think about anyone else. She's cool, and God blessed her body at every angle. We were a pretty regular thing there for a while, but then Lu and I started hanging out more often.

"So what's up baby girl?" I asked half caring.

"Nada, just thinking about you. So what happened to us? You just cut all communications on a sistah."

"I'm sorry Kenda, I've just been busy. It was nothing personal." What I should have said is I was temporarily pussy whipped.

"Humph. Well, you can apologize to me by taking me out. How bout this weekend?" She suggested.

I really am not in the mood for some sistah trying to throw it on a brother. Although, it could be a good remedy for getting my mind off of Lu Lu. You know what they say; the best way to get over a woman is to get under a new one.

"That's cool. What you got in mind Ms. Kenda?" I asked.

"Oh I don't' know. How about dinner and a movie, nothing major."

"Sounds good to me. I'll hit you up tomorrow with the details.

"Okay. Bye Vince."

It's weird how things work out. What were the odds of her calling me today? Is this a sign?

Maybe Lu Lu isn't my soul-mate after all...

Deja

"David, why are you banging on my door like you are the police or something?" I yelled. Then I remembered to stay calm. O Lord, I forgot about Derrick in the next room. I may as well get this horror show over with. Just then I heard a thump.

"What the hell was that Deja?" David was startled.

Then Derrick walked out with his keys in hand. "I'm leaving. You two need to work this out, and me being here can't help the situation." He said as he walked out the front door.

David looked as if he had seen a ghost. His mouth was hanging wide open, and he didn't move for what felt like forever.

"Was that Derrick?" He looked crazed. "What the fuck was he doing here" he asked. The looked diminished, and his eyes turned red.

"David, it's really none of your business what he was doing here. This is not your house, and I'm not about to answer questions. Especially not to you!" I said. I had my arms folded in my home girl stance. I was ready for confrontation.

He looked as if he were going to cry. A very small part of me felt sorry for him. However, a very large part of me wanted to kick his ass. "David, what did you come here to say? I really don't have the time or the patience for an argument today." I said.

"Deja, I came to tell you the truth. The entire truth." He pleaded.

"I already know the truth, I don't need you to come in here and rehash everything David. I've just now gotten to a point where I can deal with this".

"Deja, just give me a chance to tell you what has really happened".

"Go, I'm listening". I plopped down on the sofa, and he followed suit.

He went on and on about this heffah Sandy. How she lied, how she knew he was married, and how the little boy in the picture was the one he always raved about, Dante. He explained how sorry he was, and he needed me back so he could prove to me that he could be right. He explained how the affairs got easier and easier because I never cut him too much flack about it. This fool cried so hard that he threw up.

I have two words to say, bull shit.

Gabby

I have never been so embarrassed in all of my life. I can't believe his uncle called me out like that.

He was right; I used to strip at Pure Passion years ago. Being one of 3 children, I had to do what I had to do. I wanted to go to law school, but my parents could barely afford to send me to college. There was no way I could ask them to pay my way through law school.

I started working as a paralegal at a small law firm in Terre Haute. I began to struggle so much with my studies, my job, and my sanity that I didn't know what to do. That is when I became cool with my girl Sasha. She was always dressed, from head to toe during class. I figured her parents had money. She was always so laid back, while I on the other hand was falling apart.

It was terrible. My boss at the law firm, a prejudice white man, basically told me he didn't care if I was in law school. He needed me in the office more than eight hours a day in order to prep for a huge case coming up. On to of that, I still had to study. I was slowly but surely coming unglued.

To my surprise, Sasha told me she was adopted. Her adopted parents were wonderful people, but very poor. I asked her how on earth she managed to pay her way through law school, on top of dressing divalishiss on a daily basis. I hated to admit it, but I was jealous.

That same night, she took me over to Pure Passion with her. I had no idea we were going to a strip club until we pulled into the lot. I looked at her as if she had three heads. She calmly touched my hand and said, "Come with me, I want to show you something." We went in the back entrance, which told me she most definitely worked at the club. It never dawned on me that home girl was a stripper. She was so classy.

As soon as we walked into the dressing room, women began to hug and shout, "Hey Hot Cocoa!" I was surprised, yet intrigued. All the women were walking around half naked, which didn't bother me. I'm secure in my sexuality. But they seemed to act like a family. This picture was in contrast with what I saw in that movie "Player's Club". I just assumed that was the way it really was.

"Hey girl", Sasha said as she woke me out of my trance. It's amateur night tonight. You can give it a try if you want. It doesn't start for another hour, so think about it. I go on in five minutes, if you want to watch, you can go out that door right there and find a seat. There are other women out there, probably trying to steal my moves, so you won't be lonely."

I never thought about stripping. I love to practice in the mirror, but that was the extent of it. I'd always wanted to dance for a man, but never had enough courage to do it.

I walked out and found a seat. I sat alone because the only women out there looked at me like I was dessert or something. I'd hate to have to beat a heffah down for stepping to me, so I sat at the only empty table in the room. Then Sasha came out on stage. The men went wild. They were hollering and screaming. One man came right there in his seat. All the girl did was drop it and bring it back up in his face, and he came. I couldn't believe it. I felt sorry for any woman wasting her time with that brotha. I had to laugh to myself.

That's when I noticed all the attention she got. That little jealous bug started flaring up inside me. The men were damn near slobbering at the mouth. They touched her breast, but she never once allowed them to touch her below the waist. At that moment, I decided to dance for amateur hour. I ran back stage and signed up. I can dance freaky enough for this, matter of fact, it makes me feel sexy. I didn't know any of the men there, so I went for it.

I wanted to feel extra freaky before I went out on stage, so with twenty minutes until show time, I went to the restroom in a private stall. I began to play with my clit, fast, then slow. It was hard to muffle all the moans, but I maintained. I played with myself until I had an orgasm. Then I was ready.

I heard the MC announce amateur night, and I was the only girl on the list. Then he announced, "Now focus your attention, and get your sweet tooth ready for Carmel Delight!" With a fresh orgasm in tow, and no man to finish the job, I went out on stage. I found a brotha on every side of the room to focus on. A fine brotha that I could imagine being inside of me to quench the feeling I was yearning for. I worked it on that stage. It wasn't an act though. I really needed it, and I think that is what came across in my performance.

I had those men slobbering at the mouth, and screaming for more. The attention was a real rush for me. I was only on stage ten minutes, but it felt like an hour. By the time I got back stage, I was really hyped. My adrenaline was pumping. Then this tacky siren started going off in the dressing room. Sasha told me it was time for all the girls to go out. She said the real money was made with the lap dances. I was so hyped by then, I didn't second guess it.

As I ran out of the dressing room, Cole, the manager stopped me. "Alright now Carmel Delight, lap dances are only for hired personnel. Does this mean I can count on you to be here at least three nights a week?"

I stalled for a minute. "Yes, I'll be here. Where do I complete the paperwork"?

He laughed, "Baby girl, there is no paperwork. We are all independent contractors here". He laughed again and walked away. I heard him mumble under his breath "Paperwork, now that is a new one!"

I ran out on the floor and found each man I focused on while I was on stage. I worked it fast and slow, up and down. I made more in that one night, then I did all week at the law firm.

On the drive home, Sasha asked me what I thought. I told her I couldn't believe what I had just done. "Gabby, if you dance at the club three nights a week you'll make triple what you make at the law firm!"

"I know", I sighed. "I already told your boss he could count on me at least three nights a week".

"Girl, you didn't tell me that!" She smacked me a high five. I still felt a little unsure, but I really needed the money. It would also rid me of the pressure I was getting from the law firm.

And the rest was history; I stripped my way through law school. As soon as I walked across that stage at graduation, I never saw Pure Passion again. That life style had served its purpose. I then prayed to the good Lord to forgive me for what I had done. Although I did secretly enjoy stripping, I never looked back and never missed it.

I've prayed for the past five years for the Lord to send me a good man, a man like Malcolm. I thought being celibate was the right thing to do. Then the good Lord sends him, and my retched past comes back to bite me in the butt. I'll probably be single for the rest of my life.

Just my luck.

Lu Lu

I haven't heard from Vince in a few days, and it's not normal. Before our "relationship" conversation, he used to call every other day. I actually miss him. I guess he was serious about this all or nothing bit.

I want to call, but I want him to call me. A woman chasing after a man is just not cute at all. Although, it's not like I've called several times. Bug it, I'm just going to go ahead and call him.

"Hello?" He answered.

"Hey Vince, what's up?" I asked.

That's when I heard it, some heffah's voice over my man's house. What the fuck? I guess he doesn't waste any time.

"Vince, who is that?" I asked pissed off.

"Oh, that's Kenda. What's up, you need something?" He asked.

Hell to the naw. No this brotha is not playing me to the left. He had this funny tone to his voice like I was bothering him.

"Oh, well, I see you are busy."

"Yeah, I'll hit you back later." And just like that he hung up the phone.

Ouch, now that hurt. I know I had no right to be jealous, but I was. I couldn't help it.

Kenda? Humph, who the hell is she? I gotta get my mind off this shit.

Whenever your world feels it's going to crumble, you can always count on one thing, your girls!

"Gabby? It's Lu, I need a conference call. Can you call Deja?"

"Of course girl, hold on." She said. "Okay, Lu?,Deja? Ya'll there?"

"Yep" We said in unison.

"Hey Ladies, I called this conference to fill you in on what happened with Vince and I."

"What happened?" Gabby yelled.

"Calm down Gabby damn." Deja said. "What happened Lu?" She yelled just as loud as Gabby did.

"Now how you gonna yell at her and then turn right around and do the same thing Deja!" I said as we all laughed.

"Anywho. Vince told me he loved me and wanted a relationship." I said.

"And, so what's wrong with that?" Gabby said.

"I can guess," Deja laughed. "This heffah probably pulled the 'I don't believe in relationships and labels card. Am I right miss thing?" Deja said sarcastically.

"Yes I did. You know how I feel about relationships. Anyway, I called over there, and he had some heffah named Kenda there."

"Well, Lu, you didn't want him" Gabby said.

"That's the thing. I didn't think about him being with someone else. I just thought things would stay the way there were."

"Well, I guess he called your bluff Miss Thing" Deja said.

"Shut up Deja!" I laughed.

She laughed as well. "Look Lu Lu, if you love Vince, which we all know you do, then you need to quite tripping. Get up off your high horse and go get your man!" Deja yelled.

"But ya'll know how I feel about..." Gabby cut me off.

"Lu Lu! For once in your damn life, shut up and just listen. Please."

"Look Lu, we are you're girls. We aren't going to sugar coat this for you. You keep playing around, and Kenda, or whatever the hell her name is, will be walking down the aisle with your man. You'll be looking like Sanaa Lathan in that movie "Brown Sugar", watching your man marry some other woman."

We all had to laugh.

"Shit, for once I'm at a loss for words. What should I do?"

"Well," Gabby said, "You have to be a diva about this situation. Ms. Kenda is there right now, so wait until tomorrow and pull a drive by. Shit, that's how he did you right?"

"Yep." I said.

Okay, it was settled. Tomorrow I would go to Vince's house and get my man back. Just like Dianna Ross in "Mahogany".

Lord, please don't let it be too late.

Deja

I'm so confused at this point. I don't know what to do. David is filling my head with what he calls the truth. I am not quite sure if I want him or not. I'm exited about my new condo though. The thought of being "free", and not explaining my life choices to anyone is very intriguing. It's like a sense of relief. However, I also have a sense of fear. What will everyone think? I'm losing it slowly but surely.

Before a complete and total melt down, I decided to go to Derrick's house. I tried to call first, but the line was busy. I thought maybe he was on the internet, or long distance with his family. He's still a momma's boy. Knowing Derrick, he was tied up on the line with his mom and his grandma.

I jumped in my truck and high tailed it over to his house. I needed a mental break from my own thoughts. As I walked up the drive, I heard arguing in his house, and then a door slam. I started to walk away, but decided I should check on him anyway.

Just when I started to give up on anyone answering the door, it opened. I could not believe my eyes, it was Greta. The first words out of my mouth were, "Hell to the naw!" I was furious. Before I could open my mouth, I heard Derrick screaming, "What the hell are you doing answering my door, you shouldn't even be here"! Then he saw me.

I looked him square in his face, rolled my eyes, and turned to walk toward my truck. Then Derrick moved Greta out of the way and began to run toward me, "Dee wait! This isn't at all what it looks like!"

"You're not my man, you can do what you want. You don't have to explain anything to me." I smiled, but it was the most fake smile I've ever smiled.

"Deja, please don't leave. She is leaving, I want you here." He begged.

"No, you go be with your girlfriend. I'll be fine. Don't worry about me." I smiled again. Fake.

"Please Deja, let me explain. Quit trying to be calm, you know I know you. You are being so fake right now. Please get out of the truck and come inside. I swear Greta is leaving. I didn't know she was even coming. I came home and she was in my house cooking, cleaning, and answering the damn phone like she lived here. Please Deja!"

"No, you go ahead. Be with Greta. She's waiting. Besides, I'm tired of looking at her face." I said through clenched teeth. Greta was standing in the doorway watching. This was like deja vu. I can't stand that bitch.

Men, I tell you, they all have these fucked up issues. They are always caught up in some stupid situation talking about "Babe, please, this isn't what it looks like". Bull shit, it's exactly what it looks like.

Allow me to explain. Greta is this white girl that went to State with us. She graduated with Derrick. He always claimed to love me so much, but he could never quite seem to shake her. She's a rich white girl, and she probably bought all his clothes, and the pimped out mini-van he used to drive. I always suspected it was her, or the university was giving him cash on the down low. For a poor college student, he always seemed to have a lot of money.

She hated me though. We had an aerobics class together, and she and all her little red faced white girl friends used to hate a sistah. They'd be giving me the evil eye through the entire forty minute workout. I always thought it was hilarious. I caught her checking my body out a few times too. It must have been white girl envy. They all want to be built like black girls. That poor child had no ass at all!

The summer after she and Derrick graduated, he invited me back down to State for the weekend to stay with him.

The next thing I knew, here came "Suzie Homemaker" coming in the front door. I had no clue they lived together. Better yet, he lived with her. He treated her like shit. He made her leave and go back home to Bloomington for the weekend. I couldn't believe it, and the dumb heffah went too. But that was too low for me. I was furious with Derrick. That weekend was the one time I considered an actual relationship with him. In that instant, I knew it would never happen.

If he was going to be mine, he was gong to be ONLY mine. I got my bag and cut out. I flew back to Naptown. He didn't hear from me until we came back to school in the fall. He told me, as well as my roommates that he wanted to marry me, and how much he loved me. I always thought that was bullshit. He would tear up when he spoke about his love for me. He was so handsome, it would make my heart quiver, but still....BULL SHIT!

Every so often, I would see Greta leaving his suite. He always kept the white girl and her money close by. I wasn't about to play second to some rich, flat bootie, buck tooth, blonde, white girl. Not I. I may not have had any money, but I loved who I was, and I knew I would make something of myself. With or without Derrick. State's football dream.

"Deja, what are you thinking about?" Derrick shook my arm. I must have dazed off for quite a while. My truck was running, and it was in gear to drive.

"You know what? I'm tired of you, David, all men. You are all full of shit. But this is my fault. Why should I be upset with you, we had no commitment right? Just like back at State. You promised to be there for me, and you were." My eyes began to water. "Thank you Derrick".

He grabbed on tight to my truck as if he were strong enough to keep it still if I pulled off. "Deja, I swear. That woman is crazy. She's been stalking me since I left Washington. I can't get rid of her. I have a restraining order on her right now!" he yelled.

I just looked at him and shook my head. "I can't deal with this right now David, I mean Derrick". And I pulled off. I called him David on purpose, just to send a message.

As I looked back in my rear view mirror, he was just standing there with his hands on his head. I actually felt bad. I thought about what he said. Maybe the crazy heffah was stalking him.

Oh well, I have too much to deal with. I have my own damn issues.

Malcolm

I can't believe I feel like this. I only dated Gabby for a few months. I guess it's that I really felt a connection with her.

I began to daze off until I heard a knock at the door. "Who is it?"

"It's your mother, open the door".

Crap. I love my mother, but I really don't feel like being bothered today. However, she'd stand there until I opened the door, and on top of that she has a key.

"Hey Ma, what's up?"

"What's up? Did you forget our lunch date today? You Gabby, and I? I sat at the Smokey Bones Restaurant waiting on you two. We were supposed to try it for the first time together. Gabby showed up, and told me you two haven't talked since the BBQ. She apologized for not being able to stay, and then she left. Malcolm, she had tears in her eyes."

"Momma, I forgot all about that, I'm sorry. I figured you knew we would be calling that off after what happened at the BBQ".

"For what? Why would you think that Malcolm?" She looked at me with her face all squished up like I was crazy. I hated when she looked at me like that, like I was stupid or something.

"Momma!" I yelled.

As soon as those words left my mouth in that loud tone, I knew I shouldn't have done that. She got in her sistah girl stance like she was going to fight me.

"Excuse me?" she said.

"I'm sorry, I didn't mean to raise my voice." She loosened her posture. "I figured you knew. You heard Uncle. I mean damn, she used to be a stripper." I said and turned to walk toward the family room. I was disgusted, and plopped down on the couch. I could hear my mother walking behind me. She was right on my heels.

"Are you smoking crack or something?" She was back in her sistah stance. This was not going to end anytime soon. "What?" I asked.

"Gabby is a good girl, you said so yourself. She had a past before she met you. You're uncle told me that was years ago. Did you ever bother to ask Gabby what that was all about Mr. Perfect? You act like you've never done anything you should be ashamed of. Hell you've done things that even I'm ashamed of. Are you the Good Lord Jesus? Who are you to judge her past? She is an up and coming young attorney. A lot of young girls strip to make it. Hell, I'm fifty-three years old, and I know this. What is wrong with you Malcolm? You said yourself she was a gift from God." She was upset.

"Do you think God would send me a stripper?" I asked.

"She's not a stripper anymore. We are all sinners saved by grace Malcolm. What makes her sins any worse than yours?"

"Ma, she was a stripper. That doesn't bother you?"

"No, why should it? They key word here is **WAS** Malcolm. She was a stripper. The point is, what is she doing now? She's a Christian, she's faithful in her service to the Lord, she's a lawyer, she's loving, she reads to those sick babies you care so much about at the hospital. It seems to me she is a wonderful person. Did you ever think about what she is now? You did a lot of things I do not condone. If I had given up on you ten years ago, how would you feel? You were a mess then, but you are a wonderful person now. That is what matters Malcolm."

"Yeah, I guess you're right. But she was still a stripper." I said with a smile on my face. I knew I was pushing it with her.

"You know what Malcolm? You are very intelligent, but right now you are acting like a real jackass. You think about that, and I'll talk to you later. Call me when you are acting like the son I raised. I took a take out bag from Smokey Bones, enjoy." She kissed my forehead and gave me a playful smack on the cheek and off she went.

I know she was right about everything she said. It's just hard for one to admit when he is wrong. Maybe I should call her. I'm so confused.

Lord, you are going to have to help me with this one.

Vince

As I was lying on my bed staring at the ceiling, I heard a knock at the door. I swear I can never get a moment of piece.

"Who is it?" I asked.

"Who it is!" she said. I knew that was Lu Lu, although I was in a bad mood, I still had to laugh at her crazy ass.

"Hey, what's up?" She asked.

"Nothing much, just chilling, what's up with you?" I asked trying to be as nonchalant as I possibly could.

"We need to talk, can I come in or are you going to let me stand out here?" She said sounding irritated.

"Well, that's up to you. You're the one standing in the door way." I teased.

"Don't act new with me Vincent." She said flirtatiously as she walked past me into the living room.

"So what's up Lu? What brings you around my way?" I asked.

"Vince, I made a mistake." Her eyes began to water.

I was caught off guard. I'm not used to Lu Lu showing emotion like this. However, I could not let her off that damn easy. She made me feel like crap when I left her house that day. It was like s he didn't even care that I laid it all out there.

"A mistake about what Lu?" I asked as if I was irritated. But inside, I was praying that she would say the words I longed to hear.

"About not wanting a relationship. I'm afraid; I just don't want to be hurt again. But I can't just let you go, I love you Vince."

"Do you really love me, or are you just concerned about someone else having me." I chuckled.

"I'm not concerned about anyone else. Although you did play me a little cold when your girlfriend was over here."

"Girlfriend? Who? Kenda?" I had to laugh. "Girl Kenda has been around forever, and she is not my girlfriend. I just stopped hanging with her because I was so caught up with being with you all the time". I got a little angry.

"Look, I know I don't deserve a second chance, but please forgive me. I don't want to lose you Vince. Please."

"Are you sure?" I asked her.

"I've never been more sure about anything in my life. I love you, I want to be with you, and I can't live without you!" She said as she jumped on me.

"Alright, don't over do it Lu!" I laughed. She is such a drama queen. "You know I love you. I've been here for two years, why would I hurt you? Although you did hurt me the other day." I admitted.

"I know Vince. I can be so stupid. I get so stuck in my ways, and sometimes it takes a smack in the face to realize what kind of damage I've done. Please forgive me baby. I never want to see you hurt."

"I guess I can give you one more chance." I smiled.

The next thing I knew, Lu had my shirt and my pants off, and I was moaning and crying out in pleasure.

Just like Maxwell says in that song he remade, "Oh this woman's work..."

Gabby

I know the Lord sent Malcolm into my life. But I don't know how to resolve this conflict. I always knew working at Pure Passion would come back to bite me in the butt, but not like this. I thought someone at work would find out. I promised myself I would never go into politics because then I would have to worry about pictures of me dropping it like it's hot being posted on billboards all over the world.

I miss Malcolm so much. I have to be at the club tonight, and I am really not feeling it. Not without Malcolm. We've become a regular item at the club, and it won't feel the same without him there. I'm so tired of the game. Meet a man, get to know him, start to really like him, think you could possibly love him, something stupid happens, communications starts to dwindle, don't know if you are together or not because he doesn't really call anymore, then it's over. Maybe I should just get used to being alone.

I think I'm going to start job searching out of state, maybe Boston.

They say the gay population there is huge. Just my luck, I'll wind up with some confused brother. One of those men that sleep with other men, but say they aren't gay because they don't allow men to penetrate them. They are the giver, not the taker. Yep, that would be just my luck.

Just as I lie there staring at the ceiling with all of my crazy thoughts, the phone rang. The caller ID says Malcolm Brown. I instantly got butterflies in my stomach. I pulled myself together and answered the phone. "Hello? Hello? Malcolm?"

Then there was a dial tone. Now I was pissed. I dialed his number back, and the phone rang and rang until his voicemail picked up.

That's it. I'm going to the club tonight, and I'm going to have a drink. I'm not normally a drinker, but tonight, I need one. A strong one!

At the Club
Lu Lu

"Hey ladies, I've missed you gals this week. What's been up?" I asked.

"Nada!" Gabby and Deja yelled in unison.

I haven't heard from these heffah's all week. No phone calls, no e-mails, no stopping by unannounced, nothing.

Just then the DJ called us out. "Here they are ya'll, the True Diva's! Looking good as always ladies!" he yelled. I'm glad I hired him, this brother has skills. As we walked in, he started mixing the "The Men All Pause" into whatever he was playing. I had to laugh. He is a hot mess.

"Now where did he find that song!" we all laughed.

"Aw shoot, that is my theme song!" I said.

"Well ladies, Vincent is over in the corner booth waiting on me. I'm going to chat with him for a while, maybe have a drink. These shoes were not made for walking. There's plenty of room, and I've already spoken to Malcolm and Derrick, so join us when you have time." I smiled and sashayed all the way over to our booth. My feet were screaming out in pain.

You should have seen the look on those heffah's faces when I told them their men were here in the club. They think I don't know about their "issues". What they don't know is that the men have been cool since that night we were all over Derrick's house. I guess the dance they did for us that night caused some type of male bonding. They have been kicking it ever since, and Vince tells me everything.

I cracked up when the told me about Gabby being a stripper. I thought I was the only one who knew that. I went to shoot pool at the Pure Passion years ago with one of my guy friends. When I walked in the door and saw her shaking her thang on stage, I almost passed out. I couldn't believe miss goodie two shoes was stripping her way through law school. I also had a new sense of respect for her. My girl did what she had to do. And look where she is today.

I also know about Deja seeing that bitch Greta over Derrick's house. That heffah has always hated Deja. She wanted to be her. She did that shit on purpose. She'd been watching Deja go over there for a while; she knew what she was doing. It was only a matter of time. She was always jealous of the way Derrick cherished Deja. A conniving woman is a dangerous thing.

I really feel sorry for Deja. She is so confused. I've never been married, so I can't help her in that category. I think she loves David, and she doesn't want to go back in fear of what we will think. That is her husband, and I would totally respect her trying to fix her marriage. However, I also know how much she has always loved Derrick. He loves her as well, and I believe he would do anything to make and keep her happy. That is a tough situation. A love triangle.

Oh well, I guess all I can do is worry about myself. And this fine piece of dark chocolate I have sitting in this booth with me.

"Hey baby, was I gone too long?" I asked as I kissed my man. I've never been big on public displays of affection, but I guess a lot of things are changing.

Gabby

I wanted to jump up and run in the opposite direction when I saw Malcolm staring at me from across the room. I knew that look, and he wanted me to come over. Then I remembered how fly I was looking. So I stood my ground and gave him the same look

Yes indeed. I had on a slinky red dress, and at the top it was only connected by a thread on the sides. My curves showed from every angle. The front was one of those loose necks that showed the girls off just enough. I had on red open toed stilettos, and I knew I looked good. I watched him look me up and down, and then lick his lips. So in return, I looked him up and down and licked my own.

Damn he looked good. He was dressed down for a change. He had on this black shirt that buttoned up and down the front, but he had it unbuttoned. Underneath he had on a black "wife-beater", and his chest and abs made my knees weak. The jeans were this weird blue color, and they hung just right, and the belt had one of those huge Usher belt buckles. Oh yes, brotha was looking good.

But what really caught my eye were the shoes. They were black leather sandals, and he must have gotten them from out of town. They were the bomb. I could have raped this brotha. I am a total shoe fanatic.

I guessed he realized I wasn't moving, so he came over to me. He kissed me ever so gently on my cheek and said "We need to talk. You enjoy yourself, and swing by my place after the club." And just that fast, he was gone.

This man left the club. I was furious!

I better go get that drink. I really need it now.

Derrick

I guess she's going to walk around this club like she doesn't see me. She thinks she's slick, but I know her to well.

I guess I'll have to be the bigger person tonight.

"You are seriously trying to hurt some boys with that outfit tonight. Damn Deja, you look good baby." I said.

"Hmmph." Was all she had to say.

She had on a leather black mini skirt, and this shirt that had no back. I don't know how her chest stayed in place underneath it, but it was turning me on.

"Little Dee, we really need to talk."

"What is there to say? I'm still married, and you still love Greta."

"What? I've never loved Greta. You should know by now how crazy she is."

"Whatever, I have my own issues to deal with."

She started to walk away, so I grabbed her hand. Next thing I knew, we were out on the dance floor gettin our groove on.

The DJ announced that he was about to go way back. I didn't know what to expect, the DJ is young, but the brotha has skills for real.

He started playing a slow jam I didn't recognize, and mixed it into "You're Naturally Mine" by Al B. Sure. Now that was an 80's flashback. Deja and I started swaying back and forth, I wanted her right then. As I listened to the words, I knew it was meant for us. She is naturally mine; she is my soul-mate.

I was caught totally up in dancing with the woman I've grown to love even more over the years when the DJ started mixing in "Tell me when will I see you smile again" by BBD/New Edition. I can't remember which one.

That's when I realized Deja was crying. I walked her outside of the club so we could talk.

"Derrick, I need time. I don't know what to do. David is begging me for another chance. I have mixed emotions about you because of Greta. I just don't know."

"Deja, I'll be here regardless. You take your time, you know I'll always be here for you. I know we are soul-mates. I'll let destiny take control. There's no pressure here."

"Thanks for understanding Derrick. I really do love you, you know that. But I have to consider my marriage. I am a Christian woman, and I made vows. For better or worse you know?"

"I understand, but I will miss you. Does this mean I won't see or talk to you at all?" I gave her that puppy dog look.

"Now you know I can't get you out of my system that easily. I still most definitely need your friendship and advice. I'm not moving back in with David. I'm just opening the door for reconciliation."

"I got you babe. Like I said, you know I'm here for you."

We walked back into the club all smiles. You would have thought we'd won the lottery, but it was a new understanding. I was just glad she was still in my life. I knew in my heart fate would take care of the rest.

Deja

I am so glad I got a chance to see Derrick. It gave me a chance to talk to him and clear the air.

I know how crazy Greta is, and even if he was seeing her, what business was it of mine? I'm still married, and full of issues.

After the club, I decided to swing by what still felt like home to speak with David. I felt it was time.

As I pulled up in the drive, there was a red convertible I didn't recognize. I noticed the Enterprise Rental Cars sticker, so I assumed it was David's. He rents cars on a regular basis for business in close places like Chicago or Ohio. Better to put the miles on a rental, then on his own car.

I opened the front door and froze. I no longer live here, and probably shouldn't have just barged on in. I figured I may as well make my presence known.

"Hello, David, you here? It's me!" I yelled.

"Shit!" Was all I heard.

I walked into my former family room and saw David sitting on the couch with some woman. Normally I would have complimented her bomb ass haircut, but she was in the wrong place at the wrong time.

"Deja, could you sit down please?" David asked.

That's when I noticed they were both crying. I began to get nervous.

"No thanks, I'll stand. Did somebody die? Why in the hell are you two sitting here crying? Better yet, who are you?" I asked the stranger in my house.

"Deja, this is Sandy."

My heart skipped at least three beats, my mouth went dry, and I balled up my fist. I was hot. One false move, and I was prepared to beat someone down.

"What the fuck is this." I said ever so calmly.

"Deja please. Just listen." David pleaded.

"Look, you and your girlfriend have less than one minute to tell me what the fuck is going on!"

"Deja, there is no easy way around this..."

"30 seconds, you better spit it out!" At this point, I was yelling.

"Sandy is pregnant." David said as tears began to stream down his face.

My head began to spin. Those words burned my ear as if they were on fire. That was it. Deja is done. Now this is the straw that broke the camels back.

"Look David!" I had to pause and regain my composure. I can't allow him to take me there, especially in front of this bitch. "Look, you and your girlfriend have a nice life. Enjoy your new family. I can't be apart of this."

I almost felt relieved as I walked away. "Deja please!" David yelled. He jumped over the couch and grabbed me.

I looked at Sandy, and she was sitting there smiling. I refused to give her the pleasure.

"Let her go David, I can make you happy. You don't need her!" Sandy said.

No this bitch didn't.

"Look bitch, you can have him. If I were less of a woman, I'd beat your ass and his right here, but I don't have the time or the patience. Ain't no dog, I mean man, worth fighting over. Oh, and congrats. You two have fun with your new baby, and make sure my alimony payments come in on time."

David grabbed me again. I grabbed his hand, looked him directly in the eye and said, "You disgust me!"

He looked at me in total disbelieve. Like I was a total stranger. And I was, I was no longer the Deja he knew. The Deja that would bend over backward to make him happy, and would do anything to keep him. The Deja that was head over heels in love with her husband. The Deja that was always at home feeling lonely because he traveled so much.

In that instant, love turned to hate. I despised David. He truly did disgust me. The handsome face I thought he had turned ugly.

In that instant, I was free. I thought I owed it to David to try again, but he just relieved me of my obligation.

"Adios Amigos!" I yelled as I shut the front door.

As I drove down the street with my new found freedom, all I could do was laugh. "This is like some soap opera shit", I said to myself.

Then I thought about Derrick. Most would think I was rebounding, but I wasn't. I love Derrick, and I always have.

I grabbed my cell phone off the passenger seat and called him. "You feel like company Big Dee?"

"Of course, is that a trick question?" I could hear him smile through the phone.

"Well open up. I'm at your front door". I said.

It was a new since of freedom. I didn't have to feel guilty for still loving him anymore. I just wanted to be with him. I wanted to make love to him.

That's when it happened.

Derrick open the front door, I remember seeing his face. I remember hearing him yell, "Greta No!" in the most terrifying voice I've ever heard. It sounded like something off of a horror movie.

Next I felt a stinging, burning pain in my back. I fell into Derrick's arms. I noticed him crying.

All of a sudden I couldn't see, and it became increasingly hard to breathe. I heard screeching tires.

Then there was darkness...

Derrick

Deja called, and I was pumped about her visit. There was a lightness in her voice, and the sexy way she sounded when she asked if I wanted company.

I jumped up. Little did I now my worst nightmare was coming true.

I opened the front door and saw Greta drawing back with a huge knife. Before I could say anything, Deja was falling into my arms.

"Deja, No!" I cried. The only woman I loved was dying in my arms.

I applied pressure and carried her inside. I dialed 911. The minutes felt like hours passing by.

"Deja, can you hear me?" I cried.

All that came back was gurgles as blood began to pore out of her mouth.

"No Deja, no, please, stay with me baby!"

My chest began to tighten and burn. I felt like life was slipping away from me as well. I've never been so scared in all of my life.

Just then the ambulance arrived. They wouldn't let me ride, so I jumped in my truck. I ran every red light and stop sign.

As I paced back and forth in the hospital, I called the team's transportation service and put in an order to pick up Lu Lu and Gabby. I knew they would be in no condition to drive once I called them.

I dialed Lu first. "Lu, hey this is Derrick. Can you get Gabby on three-way?"

"Yeah, what's wrong? You sound weird Big Dee."

"Just get Gabby on the phone Lu, please." I didn't mean to yell at her, but this was urgent.

"Okay, hold on."

There was no easy way to tell them what happened; I knew they would flip out.

"Hello Gabby, Derrick, you both there?"

"Yes" We said in unison.

"Okay, what's wrong Derrick, you are scaring me!" Gabby said.

"I'm not quite sure what happened, but Greta stabbed Deja, she is in emergency right now. I sent the transportation service for both of you, so get dressed."

"Hold on, the driver is at my door right now. Gabby, get ready, we'll be there in five minutes!" Lu Lu screamed as the hung up the phone.

"Okay, Derrick call me right back!" Gabby yelled.

I dialed her number. "Gabby? It's me. Calm down."

"What the hell happened, I swear I will kill that heffah when I see her."

"I know, the detectives have already questioned me. I swear I can't believe this. All I saw was Greta run up behind her, and I was too late to stop it. It happened so fast. Gabby, this is all my fault. I knew Greta was crazy, but I never thought that..." I began to cry and couldn't complete my own sentence.

"Derrick, calm down sweetie. This is not your fault. Greta is insane, there's no way you could've known she would go to this level. The car just pulled up, we are on our way!"

Gabby

"Hello, Malcolm?"

"Hey Gabby, you on the way?" He asked.

"Look, I know I said I was coming over, but Deja's been stabbed. We are on our way to the hospital right now.

"Oh my Lord! What hospital Gabby?"

"Methodist"

"I'm on my way, I'll meet you there."

I am a nervous wreck. I don't know how serious the stab is, but Derrick sounded terrified. I don't want to lose Deja, we can't lose Deja. Oh Lord, give me strength.

"Lu Lu, what are we going to do? We can't lose Deja?" I began to cry uncontrollably.

"Gabby, she'll be okay. We have to be strong. We have to be strong for Deja okay?" She sounded convincing until she began to cry harder than I was.

We hugged in an attempt to console one another, but it felt awkward.

One of us was missing...

David

Who in the hell could be calling me now. I'm furious, and I'm not in the mood to be bothered.

"Hello!" I yelled.

"Hey David Man, this is Derrick".

What the fuck, why in the hell is this negro calling my house? His nuts must be the size of bowling balls for calling here.

"What?" I asked. Not really caring.

"Look man, I know you are wondering why I'm calling. Deja is in the hospital, she's been stabbed. You need to get down here right now."

I fell to my knees. It felt like someone punched me in the gut and knocked all the wind out of me. Lord, help me please. I know I've done irreparable damage to my marriage, but please let Deja pull through this.

"David, man, do I need to send a car for you? You shouldn't be driving."

"No, I'll be okay. I'll be there in ten minutes." I said still stunned.

I pray that Deja will be okay, I really do. However, I can't get the feeling of jealousy out of my mind. How is it that Derrick knew this before me. Why is he in the picture so strong all of a sudden?

I snapped out of my thoughts and grabbed my keys.

"Baby, where are you going?" Sandy asked.

"Just get the hell out of my house. This is all your fault!" I knew it was just as much my fault as hers, but I needed someone to blame.

"What? I didn't make this baby by myself. You were the one married; I came into this a single woman!" She smiled.

"You conniving bitch!" I said as I ran towards her. Her eyes got as big as saucers. I wanted to strangle her ass, but I caught myself.

I've never hit on a woman, and I'm not going to start now. I slowly began to walk away.

"Just get the fuck out of my house. I want you gone before I get back." I said as I slammed the door.

I heard her yell. "Don't worry boo, I know you're upset. But I still love you! I'll be here, in your house, waiting!"

That heffah is crazy. I can't believe I've gotten myself wrapped up in this fatal attraction shit.

Lu Lu

"I am a nervous wreck. Derrick, when was the last time the doctor came out to give an update?" I asked.

"They haven't, that is what is driving me insane over here." Derrick said as he paced back and forth.

That's when we heard the page for the Deja Smith party. We all ran towards the doctor.

"What's going on with Deja? Is she okay?"

"May I ask who you are sir? Are you her husband, we noticed the ring?" the doctor asked.

"No, I'm a close friend. What..." he cut Derrick off mid sentence.

"I'm sorry, I can only speak with immediate family sir. Is there any immediate family here?"

"Hey Dr. Medford. Her immediate family is on the way. Could you give me the update please? I will act as a liaison?" Malcolm said.

I completely forgot he worked here at the hospital. Thank you Lord for putting the right people, in the right places, at the right time.

"Oh sure, I didn't see you Malcolm." She said. She pulled Malcolm off to the side. We waited anxiously. I couldn't take it anymore. As soon as I was about to bust up the conversation, the doctor smiled and walked away.

"Okay guys, sit down." Malcolm said calmly. One could tell he did this for a living.

"She pulled through surgery, but she lost a lot of blood. The stab destroyed one of her kidneys, but she is a strong girl. She can live with only one. She lost consciousness, and has yet to regain it. They can't explain why, but she is still in a coma." Malcom said as one tear slid down his cheek.

We all hugged one another. "Lord, please give us the strength to be strong for Deja." I prayed.

"Did she say when we can go in and see her?" I asked. My hands were visibly shaking.

"Yes, we can go in now." Malcolm said.

"Hey baby, what happened, what's going on?" Vincent said as he came running into the emergency room.

"Vincent!" I was so relieved to see him. I stood on my toes to speak softly in his ear.

"Deja was stabbed by Greta. We're going in to see her now, come on." I grabbed his hand. I needed to feed off of his strength.

As we walked into Deja's room, it felt as though the air was sucked out of my lungs. She had tubes coming from what seemed like every hole in her body. I couldn't believe it. I think everyone else felt the same way. The tears were flowing all over the room.

The weird thing was, tears were coming from Deja's eyes as well. "Malcolm" I whispered. "I thought they said she was in a coma. She's crying. And look, she opened her eyes a little".

"That's normal Lu" Malcolm said. "You don't have to whisper. I believe it is healthy for coma patients to hear the voices of their loved ones. It's normal for them to open their eyes and cry. No one knows for sure, but I believe they want to wake up and speak when they hear their loved ones voices, but they can't. Therefore, they cry."

At that moment, Gabby and I began to cry uncontrollably. I stroked Deja's hands and spoke to her.

"You look here heffah, you go ahead and get all the rest you need." I put her hand up to my face. "But you are going to wake up. Do you hear me? You are going to wake up?"

"We just have to make sure we keep communicating with her. She needs to know there are people here at all times." Malcolm said as he hugged Gabby.

Just then David walked in the room. He looked around, and then at Deja. Before he could hit the ground, Vincent and Derrick caught him, and sat him down in a chair.

"David, David!" I yelled.

"I'm okay Lu Lu. I wasn't prepared to see her like this. What happened?"

Malcolm introduced himself and pulled David into the hallway to explain.

David came back in the room and began to speak to Deja. He grabbed her hand, "Deja, it's David. I am so sorry for everything that has happened. I love you. Please pull through this." He began to cry.

He then got up, and left.

"David, where are you going?" I ran out behind him.

"I can't do this Lu Lu. I've done so much damage to Deja, I just can't take it". He said.

"Be careful David." I said. He threw up his hand and off he went.

Derrick

"You found her? Did you lock her up?" I asked the Detective.

"Yes, she is in custody. She confessed to stabbing Deja, but she said it was your fault."

"Excuse me?" I asked

"Yeah, she's a real nut case. She said she had to get rid of her because she was in the way, and you couldn't focus."

"So what's going to happen?"

"Well, we have your statement. If we need anything else, we'll be in touch".

"Thank you detective."

As I walked back into the room I saw all the people that cared about Deja standing at her bed side. She's very fortunate to have such wonderful friends.

Her parents passed away years ago in a car accident, but she never complains about that. She always said, "Don't feel sorry for me, God only sends you angels for so long."

"Hey guys, I just spoke with the detective. They caught Greta, and she confessed. It appears to be an open and shut case."

"Good, better them catching her then me. I swear, if I'd have gotten my hands on that bitch, I would have tried to kill her!" Gabby yelled.

Then a raspy voice said, "Calm down Ms. Thing, you're too cute to be trying to fight."

We all jumped up and ran over to her bed. She sounded weak, but that was most definitely her.

"Deja, how do you feel baby? It's good to have you back!" I smiled and kissed her on the forehead.

"I feel groggy, and I hurt all over." She began to cough. "My mouth is dry, can a sistah get something to drink?" "I got you Deja!" Malcolm jumped up and ran out to the nurse's station.

"Can somebody tell me exactly what happened to me?"

I gave her the short version of what happened with the stabbing. I then explained what happened as far as her surgery.

"So, I only have one kidney? Is that okay?" She asked.

"Yes baby, they said you could live with one kidney just fine. Besides, if something were to happen, I'd just give you one of mine."

She laughed, but I could tell it hurt.

"Uhm. I think someone should call David and let him know Little Dee is awake." I announced.

"Why? Don't call him. Let him go home to his pregnant girlfriend." Deja laughed.

"What? Are you serious?" Lu Lu stood up.

"Yep, he told me she was pregnant, and I am through. I was headed over to Derrick's for a 'celebration' of my new freedom before all of this happened."

"You've got to be freakin' kidding me" Gabby said.

"Nope, I'm for real. And to top that off, his girl was sitting there when he told me".

"Deja, we still need to call him. He didn't look good when he left here." I advised.
"Whatever, I'm too sleepy to worry about it" She said in a very low voice.

Before we knew it, she was fast asleep.

All I could say was, "Thank you Jesus!"

Deja

When my friends explained what happened to me, I couldn't believe it. That crazy bitch Greta could've killed me. She's crazier than I thought.

But I'm still here! The Lord has truly blessed me with a second chance. Life is too short to play around.

I get to go home today, and I am so glad because this hospital food is about to drive me insane. I'm on the borderline of being anorexic up in here.

"Hey Little Dee, you ready to go home?" Derrick woke me out of my trance. "What were you so deep in thought about?" He asked.

"Oh nothing, just that I want some King Ribs on the way home. I can't eat this hospital food another day!" I was frustrated, and so was my stomach.

"You sure you're up to stopping? I should probably take you straight home. Then I can go back out and get you some ribs" he said, sounding so sincere.

"Look Big Dee", I was rolling my neck at this point. "I'm fine. Don't start treating me like I'm disabled, or I will have to re-think letting you stay with me." I got in my sistah girl stance.

"You couldn't kick me out even if you tried, and you can unfold your arms and stop rolling your neck." He said mocking me. He looked ridiculous trying to roll his neck.

"Whatever!" I yelled. He cracked me up. "Actually, I wanted to talk to you seriously." I said, changing the mood.

"What up? You know you can talk to me about anything." His face softened.

"I'll wait until we get in the car."

Just then the Medical Assistant came in the room with a wheel chair.

"Are you ready to go home missy?" She asked with a smile.

"I sure am." I was so happy to get out of there.

"I'm going to go to the garage and pull the truck around" Derrick said as he kissed my forehead.

"You've got yourself a real looker! Doesn't he play for the Colt's?" She asked.

"Yes, he does, and yes I do have myself a good one. Thank you!" I said as she rolled me down the hall.

I didn't realize how much pain I was actually in until I attempted to climb up into Derrick's Range Rover. I grimaced one good time before Derrick immediately swooped me up and gently placed me in the passenger seat of the truck. I could see right then he was going to treat me like a big baby, and work my last damn nerve.

I must admit it felt good though.

As soon as I walked in my condo, there were flowers and homemade cards from my third grade class at the academy.

I immediately teared up. I miss my class, and I know they are giving the sub a hard time. I'm going to have to make a rapid recovery.

"So Deja, what did you want to talk about?" Derrick asked.

"Look baby, what just happened really put a lot of things into perspective for me. I realize that I could've died, and life is too short.

While I was out of it, I don't think I was in a coma, it was weird I couldn't hear anyone else but I could hear you. I could hear you speaking to me Derrick. I remember every word you said. It was like I was in the fog, and the only thing keeping me safe was the sound of your voice. I know without a doubt that you are my soul-mate. I know we were meant to be together."

"I contacted a lawyer and had him visit me in the hospital. David will be served with divorce papers at the end of next week."

"What are you saying Deja?" He said. His eyes began to water.

"Derrick, if you start crying I will too, and I won't be able to finish what I'm trying to say!" I laughed.

"I'm not crying, I'm misting, men don't cry!" He had to laugh at himself.

"Anyway. I'm not saying we have to get married right now, I'm just saying that I love you. I need you in my life Derrick. I want to be with you and only you. I don't want to play this game anymore. We've been playing it since we were at State." I took a deep breath.

"Deja, I have waited for more than a decade to hear you say just that. I personally don't care about your marriage/divorce. I would marry you right now if you'd let me. I've loved you since the first time I laid eyes on you walking across campus. That is why I stayed single. I've never loved anyone else."

"Derrick, I'm so happy you feel this way!" Then he kissed me so passionately I believe I had an orgasm.

"Deja?" He startled me.

"Huh?" my eyes were still closed.

"You complete me, and you had me at hello!" We both cracked up laughing.

"You are so crazy! Don't make me laugh like that, I may burst my stitches!"

After that, there was nothing more to say. We lay in my in my bed and held one another. I heard Derrick began to breathe deeply and snore. As he held me, I realized, I've never felt as secure as I did in that moment.

Malcolm

"Hey Gabby, what took so long?" I asked as she hung her coat in the hall closet.

"I'm sorry. I was over Deja's cleaning and cooking dinner so it would be there when Derrick brought her home. I must have lost track of time."

"No, don't apologize. We all need to chip in and help her get well." I said.

"You know we need to talk right?" I asked. She looked like she could throw-up.

"Yes, I've been avoiding the subject." She admitted.

"First off, I'd like to apologize to you Gabby."

"For what?" She asked confusingly.

"I had no right to judge you. It was wrong of me to stop calling. Your past is just that, in the past."

"But I can explain Malcolm" she said as she put her hand on my thigh.

"No, there's no need to explain. I love you for who you are now. I don't care about anything before that."

"Are you sure Malcolm?"

"Yes. I love you. I know it hasn't been a long time, but I know the Lord sent you to me. I've prayed for a God fearing, loving, giving, Christian woman. And that is exactly what he sent me. Thank you Jesus! You just have to forgive me for not seeing my blessing after that incident. That was nothing but the devil."

"Malcolm, thank you. And I love you too." She began to cry, so I kissed her.

Then kissing turned into groping, next thing I knew, I was lying on top of her in the middle of the floor.

"Malcolm, we shouldn't!" She said. However, she didn't stop me.

I began to kiss her all over while removing her clothes. I fasted sexually for more than a year waiting for the Lord to send me the right one, and I know I found her in Gabby. I could hold back no longer.

As I kissed her in the center of her body, she began to tremble. I flipped her over and began to kiss her shoulders and all the way down her back. I could tell by the deep arch in her back, she thoroughly enjoyed that.

Next, I turned her back over and lovingly kissed her breasts. She began to beg me for it. "Malcolm, I need you." She whispered.

Little did she know, my body ached for her as well. I've waited so long for this woman. I didn't know who she was at that time, but Gabby is everything I prayed for. Like the song says, "I loved her from conception".

I picked the love of my life up off the floor and carried her to my bedroom. I gently laid her down.

"Malcolm please!" she begged.

At that point I couldn't wait another minute. I entered her body, she was so wet, and so warm.

Then we became one...

David

I know she probably doesn't want to talk to me, but I have to call and see how she is doing. I feel like shit, I look like shit, I guess I am shit. In five years, I've never called in sick to work. I haven't been to the office in over a week. My damn admin keeps calling here like I died or something.

Bug it, I'm calling.

"Hello?" Deja said. She sounds so happy.

"Hey Deja, it's me, David".

"Oh, hello, can I help you?" She asked as if I was a stranger. She sounded normal, and that really hurt. I guess I expected her to sound as terrible as I felt.
"I got the divorce papers. They are sitting here in front of me. Are you sure this is what you want?" I asked

pathetically. I knew I sounded pathetic and tired, but I didn't care.

"David, we don't have to make this hard. It is for the best, and you know it. You are obviously not ready for a committed relationship, and that's okay. But you need to be honest with yourself." She said lightly. It's was almost like it wasn't even a big deal to her.

"Deja, why do you sound so flippant? It's like this doesn't even bother you. Don't you love me?" I whined. I was even beginning to make myself sick.

"Sweetie look, you really hurt me. You've broken my heart into so many pieces; I thought it was not repairable. And this last incident was not the first time. I refuse to allow myself to turn into an ice queen because of what you've done. You made your bed, and now you have to lie in it." She said matter of factly.

"I know, I really just wanted to make sure you were okay, but then I got the divorce papers, and I didn't know what to do." I said.

"Sign them. It's that simple. Sign them, and then thank the Lord we don't have children. That would make this entire situation a huge mess. I tried to love you David, I really did, but you threw my love away. You need to find out what your problem is and fix it. You need to get back into church, and allow the Lord to help you. Next, you need to help Sandy through this. She can't raise that child alone, and no matter how upset you are, she didn't make that baby by herself. You can only be mad at yourself. No matter how terrible things may seem, you will live."

"I love you Deja. I really do. I know I've done you wrong, but I do love you. I just want you to know that. What I've done is truly tearing me apart inside. I'll sign the papers, but I honestly don't want a divorce."

"David, you may be torn apart inside, but I think that is nothing compared to the way I've felt. Thank you for signing the papers, and not making this difficult. You take care now." She said.

And just like that, she was gone. No attachments, no children, no reason to ever hear from her again.

There are no words that could explain the hurt I feel right now.

Only death could compare.

Gabby

I was so relieved when I went over Malcolm's the other day. The entire time Deja was in the hospital, I was as sick as a dog. Malcolm was there everyday. Going on as if nothing had happened, but I knew the day was coming that we had to have "the" talk.

I could've killed his uncle for even bringing it up.

I had this entire speech prepared about why I was a stripper. A real sob story. However, I never got a chance to utter a word of it.

He told me he was no longer concerned with my past, and that he loved me. Next thing I knew, we were making love. I've waited so long to be with this man, or any man. Let me tell you, it was worth the wait!

Just when I thought he was through with me, and I'd lost him for good, he let me know he was here to stay. He said the past is in the past, and he loves me for who I am today. Did you read what I just said? He said he LOVES me.

Then we made love. It was so slow and passionate. Every time I think about it I get a chill. It was the most loving experience I'd ever had with a man. It's too good to be true. I can't believe it.

Either God has truly blessed me, or I am in big trouble. Just my luck he is crazy or something.

Just my luck.

Saturday Night at True Diva's
Deja

It is so good to be out and about again. I swear I was losing my mind. I was one step away from killing Derrick too. He wouldn't let me lift a finger. He had the nerve to get mad at a sistah for driving to the grocery store while he was at practice.

I gotta give it to him though. He is so sweet, and patient. He has been there every step of the way for me, emotionally and physically. Through my stabbing and through my divorce. For the first time in over ten years, I truly believe that he loves me.

Anywho, we are in the club tonight. The DJ just announced us as we walked in.

"I tell you, with that dude, we can't even sneak in the club" I laughed.

"Nope, but you know me, I like a grand entrance." Lu Lu said.

"You are sick Lu", Gabby laughed.

"Look over there at that table full of fine ass men", I said as I gazed over at the VIP section. There sat Vince, Derrick, and Malcolm looking all lovalishiss.

"Damn. We sure are some blessed sistah's. When was the last time we all had men, at that same time that actually got a long. And on top of that, they understand our friendship." Gabby said.

"I know, I am truly happy." Lu said with her head tilted to the side gazing at our men.

What? I can't believe my eyes or my ears. I never thought I would live to actually see the day that Lu Lu would be acting this way. She is truly in love! I am so excited for her.

"So ladies, who will be married first?" I asked, "Because I know it won't be me!" I laughed.

"What? Derrick would marry you today if he could Deja." Gabby said.

"I know, but it wouldn't be right for me to marry so soon would it?" I asked. Although deep inside, I knew for a fact that I want to marry Derrick, I was really trying to see how they felt about it.

"Girl, life is too short to be worried about what other people think. Follow your heart and pray to the Lord. What is HE telling you to do?" Lu Lu said.

"What!?" Gabby and I both yelled in unison.

"I know, but don't be shocked. Almost losing Vince has totally changed my attitude. That was a real reality check." She admitted.

"You sure needed one miss thing." I laughed.

"Whateva heffah." She laughed.

"Well, I'm just elated to have all three of us here, together again!" Gabby said as she hugged me tightly.

"Don't start Gabriel! You will have all of us crying up in here!" I said as I hugged her in return.

It truly was good to be back to my old self again. All I could do was thank the Lord for pulling me through.

"Bring ya'lls fine asses over here!" Vince yelled at us. I guess we were stuck in our own little world. You know how girl friends get; we can turn a five minute conversation into two hours. We could have our coats on, ready to leave, and one person will start talking. Next thing you know, we are standing at the front door sweating because we stood there for over an hour laughing about something.

Girlfriends. I don't know how a woman could get a long with out her girls. It's a blessing to have them.

Thank you Jesus for blessing me with two beautiful girlfriends.

"Let's dance ya'll. I'm in the mood to celebrate!" I yelled.

Next thing you know we were all on the dance floor. The DJ was playing R Kelley's "Happy People". We stepped and laughed and laughed and stepped. Gabby had us doing this partner switch step she learned in Chicago. It was like a hip square dance. We had so much fun.

By the time we got off that dance floor, the club was closing down and the DJ had just announced the last song. My hair was as flat as a pancake, and I could no longer feel my toes. I had to take my shoes off, the man-killers were killing me!

"Oh girl, that is my jam!" I said. The DJ started playing "Always and Forever". I hadn't heard that song in so long.

That is when it happened.

Malcolm was down on one knee, then Derrick, then Vince.... All three of them had there arms extended with ring boxes in hand...

What in the hell?

Then the DJ announced, "I need everyone's attention, don't leave yet ya'll....True Diva's, Gabriel Ann, Deja Janet, and Lolita Lynn.....these gentlemen would like to know if you would do them the honor of being there wives?"

I almost fainted. I couldn't believe this. I mean what? I can't breath. I had to catch Gabby, she almost tripped over her own two feet.

Before I could even blink, Lu Lu screamed, "YES!" and was hugging and kissing Vince. Next Gabby was crying so much it was funny, then she started jumping up and down, yelling "Yes, yes, yes, yes, yes", and she began hugging and kissing Malcolm.

I didn't realize I was still standing there, and Derrick was still down on one knee with the most beautiful diamond ring staring up at me. The song changed, and the DJ was playing "Yearning for Your Love" by the Gap Band. Then he said, "Alright Ms. Deja Janet, what is it going to be homegirl?"

Derrick looked up at me again with tears in his eyes. Then I snapped back to reality. "Lord, what should I do?" I prayed silently. Then just like that, it came to me. I almost lost my life, and any chance at being with this man. The man I have always loved. I'm divorced, and I'm grown. I can do what I want. Then I asked myself, "What does Deja want?"

And then I answered myself, "Deja wants Derrick!"

"Yes, Yes, I would love to be your wife, Yes!" I screamed. The whole crowd began to cheer.

"Baby, you made me nervous, I thought you were going to say no" he said as he stood up to hug and kiss me. He swooped me up and we began to kiss passionately.

I can not even comprehend what just happened. This is unreal. The only thing I could think of to say was...

Thank you Lord!

Lu Lu

I am still in dream land over what happened at the club last week. I am officially engaged. Me, the one who thought she would never be married. I had no clue they were all planning this. I get chills just reliving that moment in my head.

Then I heard someone jiggling keys in the front door. Must be one of the girls, they are the only one's with keys. I guess I'll have to give Vince one now. My fiancé. I still get giggly like a little school girl when I say that word. Fiancé.

"Lu, you ready?" Gabby yelled.

"Yeah girl, I'm in the bedroom!"

"Hurry up heffah!" I heard Deja yell. "We got a lot to do".

We were on our way to every bridal store in the state of Indiana. Knowing us, we'll probably hit up Chicago as well. We had three weddings to plan, and very little time to do it. Vince and I are getting married in June, Gabby and Malcolm in August, and Deja and Derrick in October. We decided it would be cost efficient if we picked the same wedding colors. We pretty much have the same taste anyway. That way, our bridesmaids could wear the same dresses in each wedding. Not to mention we would all be maids of honor in each others weddings, so this would save time and money.

"Ladies, this still feels like a dream. Can you believe they proposed to all three of us at the same time? I know I keep saying it, but I just can't believe it. And they have become so close." Gabby said.

"Well, I consider it a blessing. This way they understand how close we are, and they won't have a problem with it. You know how some women get married, and their hubby's don't want them around their friends anymore." I said.

"Whose cell phone is that ringing, is that me?" I asked.

"Nope, it's me." Deja said as she grabbed her purse.

The next thing I knew, she was falling to the ground. "Turn on the news." She said in the weakest voice I've ever heard her use.

I ran to the television and hit channel 13. I always watch them because Lindsey Davis is my cousin. Not to mention they have the more African American reporters than any other station. When the flashed over to Lindsey, she was reporting on a plan crash outside of California.

"Deja, what is it, what is going on?" Gabby yelled.
Deja began to cry. "This is so unfortunate." She said as she began to cry harder.

I immediately got nervous. I knew Derrick was away at a training camp with the Colt's. Please Lord tell me he didn't fly. Where did Deja say he was? Did he fly to Chicago?

"What is it? Who was on that plane?" I yelled. I began to get impatient.

"That was David's flight, there were no survivors." She said softly.

"What?" I yelled and began to cry myself.

"And Sandy is in labor, that was David's mother on the phone." She said as she pulled herself up off the floor. "She's on her way to California to be with Sandy." She added.

"What are you going to do?" Gabby asked.

"Well, there first thing I'm going to do is pray."

We all held hands and began to call on the strength of the Lord. We prayed for a very long time. We shouted, and asked the Lord to have mercy on his soul....and to welcome him into his mighty kingdom. I'd never cried so hard in all my life. We prayed and cried so long and hard, I had no tears left to shed.

"...In the mighty and powerful name of Jesus, Amen." Deja said.

"Amen." Gabby and I echoed.

"Okay, there's no more we can do. Now we need to go on with our lives. We have appointments to keep ladies, let's get shopping!" Deja yelled as if she found new strength.

"Deja, are you sure you still want to do this?" I asked.

"Yeah Deja, we understand if you don't." Gabby added.

"Look ladies, I feel terrible about what happened to David, but it is out of our hands. We gave it to the Lord, and that is where it needs to stay. I am no longer his wife, his mother will handle things. And she knows if she needs help, I am here. Right now, Sandy is the one that needs help, but that is not my place either. I will give all the money from his life insurance to her child because I am still the beneficiary. And I am sure that WE will attend the funeral correct?" She asked.

"Of course!" Gabby and I said in unison.

"Then it is done. I'm still getting married to Derrick, his death doesn't change anything. However, I will always feel a small emptiness with him gone, but that is normal with any death. Let's go ladies. I'm hungry." She said.

"Well Lil Dee, I admire your strength." I admitted.

"Honey, I'm shaken, but there's nothing I can do to change what has happened." She said. "Okay ladies, let's go plan our weddings!"

"Okay, let's do it!" Gabby yelled.

Deja

I can't believe what has happened. I tried to be strong for Gabby and Lu, but I am crushed.

I truly do not second guess my decision to marry Derrick, but I am in total disbelief about what has happened to David. It feels weird. I feel like I should be doing more to assist with the arrangements, but it is not my place.

That was confirmed yesterday. I drove over the David's mother's house to see if there was anything I could do. When I walked in, Sandy was sitting there with the baby. She didn't have the same smirk on her face that I was accustomed to. I actually felt sorry for her. She had to raise that child alone after all.

She did apologize to me. I told her there was no need for an apology and that I was sorry for her lose. It felt weird to say it, but it was true. He was her man, not mine.

I spoke with his mother, and she explained that David told her what happened, and she was sorry. She said she would always love me and consider me her daughter, but she had to help Sandy in anyway she could. She didn't want her grandchild to grow up not knowing her. She also told me Sandy put in for a transfer with her company, and would by living here in Indy.

I told her I loved and missed her, and if she needed anything to feel free to call. And then I left. No reason to ever return. I was no longer apart of that family.

While I felt relieved, I still felt a sense of loss. I prayed silently...

"I'll miss you David. See you when I get there".....and that was that.

Malcolm

"Dog, ya'll got to be there on time. What are you doing still at that office? Alright, Lu Lu is going to hurt you if you miss this appointment. Alright man, I'll see you there."

Vince and Lu Lu are getting married next month, and we are just now getting fitted for the tuxes. I hate doing things at that last minute, but none of our schedules would permit anything sooner. Derrick has been in and out of different training camps, Vince's job sent him to Africa, and we have three nurses on maternity leave. It must be in the water at that hospital. I'm a man, and I'm scared to drink it. If one more of those women get pregnant, I'm going to scream.

I enjoy flashing back on that night at the club. The girls were in a state of shock. They had no idea we'd been planning to propose to them for a while. Ever since Deja left the hospital, we've been looking for the perfect rings for our "True Divas".

I've never been big on close friends, but Vince and Derrick are cool people. We kick it quite often, it's pretty much become routine. Now I understand why Gabby raves about her girlfriends so much.

Not to mention, kickin' it with Derrick has its benefits. We get free tickets to all the NFL football games. Vince has benefits as well. He is a marketing manager for the Pacers Franchise. So we get free tickets to all the NBA games too.

We always have a ball hanging out. I also enjoy hanging at the club. We got the finest women in the State of Indiana, and they own the hottest club. I tell you, I've only been living here a year, and I got all the hookups.

But we are all going to pay if we don't make this tux fitting. I'm sure Lu Lu is crazy enough to kill us all.

A few weeks ago, we were chillin over Derrick's crib discussing this wedding business. Vince admitted he had cold feet. We were all relieved to hear that. I think it is normal for a man. Then Derrick asked us two questions that put it all into perspective.

"Man ya'll tripping. I don't have cold feet. I know for a fact I want to marry Deja, not a doubt in my mind!" He said.

"Man, how is that. How can you be so sure you want to spend the rest of your life unquestionably with this one woman?" Vince said.

"It's easy. You have to ask yourself first; if you left her, and saw her out with another man, how would you feel? And secondly; if she died, could you live?" He said matter of factly.

"Man, I would want to kill a nigga if I saw him with Lu, and if something were to happen to her, I would probably mourn myself to death. The only thing that could keep me alive would be Jesus himself." Vince laughed.

"Dog, if something were to happen to Gabby, I don't know what I would do. And I don't even want to think about seeing her with another man. I think I'd have to move to another state!" I laughed.

"Exactly." Derrick said laughing. "Ya'll know I almost lost Deja, and I'll be damned if I allow her to slip through my fingers. As long as we both have breath, I will be there for her. Life is to short for maybe's dog. Maybe she's not the one, maybe she'll get on my nerves, maybe I'm making a mistake. You have to live life each day like it could be your last. Greta's crazy ass taught me that lesson" he explained.

"Man, you are right. Shit, I'm getting all choked up over her" Vince laughed.

"Man, don't start no crying. Although, my brother is correct. If I had second thoughts before, I most definitely don't have them now. Thanks man." I said.

We all gave each other some dap, and laughed at Vince while he tried to wipe a tear out of his eye.
"Man, forget ya'll" Vince laughed.

Yep. When you can cry in front of your boys, you are most definitely homies. But thank God it was him and not me!

Gabby

"Oh Lu Lu! You look so beautiful in that dress. I think I am going to cry. I really like that one!" I said.

"No, Gabby, I like the one you have on. That is a bad dress. That is so beautiful." Lu said.

"Well, maybe you two should switch. And since nobody seems to like mine, I am putting it back." Deja frowned.

"Hmmm. No, I don't like that one Lil Dee. You should get something that is longer. I don't like the ones that stop mid calf. Gabby, if you don't like yours I want it. Do you want mine?" Lu Lu said.

"Yes, give me yours, I don't like the way this one fits. I don't have enough breasts to fill it up. I want something that will push me up, you know, make it look like I have cleavage."

"You could always get it altered Gabby." Deja said.

"Nope, I don't want to go through all of that, I want my dress to fit right now. Didn't you see Judge Judy when that alterations shop ruined the girls dress the day before the wedding? That would be just my luck." I said.

I don't want anything to ruin my wedding day.

"Will you guys quit fussing? I'm ready to get......" Lu was talking and all of a sudden she fainted. She hit the ground before we could even comprehend what was happening.

"Lu Lu! What is wrong? Somebody dial 911!" I yelled.

"No, Lu Lu, no, wake up sweetie, come on..." Deja yelled.

"No, stop, don't dial 911. I'm okay, I just got light headed." Lu Lu said groggily.

"Did you eat? Are you on your period? You know you have low iron, you have to eat Lu" Deja said all in one breath.

"I'm okay, I just got light headed like I said." Lu Lu said angrily. "Please don't fuss over me you guys, let's just keep shopping".

"No, we are going to the hospital." I demanded.

"No, I'm not. I will call my doctor on Monday." Lu Said.

"Are you sure Lu Lu, you really scared us." Deja said.

"Positive. Just give me some chocolate. I know you have some in your purse Gabby." Lu Lu laughed.

"I never leave home without it". I said.

Lu Lu

With the wedding planning and everything else, I completely spaced the fact that I have yet to come on my period. It hadn't even dawned on me until Deja said something in the bridal store. I can't believe I fainted. I can not stand not having total control of myself. And I surely can't stand those two fussing over me. I'm the momma here.

I get married in less than a month, and I think I am pregnant. I can't believe this. I can not believe this. I need to be sure.

Well, I hope these EPT tests are as accurate as they claim to be. This has been the longest two minutes I've ever spent in my life. I can't believe this. I am in total disbelief.

Well here goes nothing...

Two lines, what does that mean? Where are those instructions?

I began to read out loud, "Two lines equals pregnant, one line equals not pregnant".

Yep, pregnant. Damn.

Lord, help me please...

Deja

"What are ya'll heffahs doing coming by here unannounced. I could have been butt naked doing the whop right here in the living room." I laughed.

"Well, you weren't. Thank the Lord because I don't want to see no mess like that!" Gabby laughed. "This crazy girl woke me up, before noon on a Saturday, talking about we need an emergency exhale party. And ya'll know it is too damn early to be talking about anything. I can't even comprehend what is going on. Who am I, why am I out of my bed, what time is it?" Gabby wailed as she flopped down on the sofa.

"Anyway, you are so overly dramatic!" Lu Lu laughed. "I called this emergency meeting for a reason". She said as she handed both of us a colored piece of paper.

"Lu Lu! Is this what I think it is?" I asked as my eyes began to water.

"Lu, oh Lu Lu...." Gabby began to cry and hug me.

Lu Lu just handed us pictures from her first ultra-sound.

She sighed and said, "I went to the doctor, and I'm already 3 months pregnant. I had no clue. I know this is the first month I missed my cycle, but what the Lord wants he gets."

"Have you told Vince?" I asked. I knew Derrick hadn't told me anything, and I know he is no good at holding this kind of juice.

"No, I'm going over there this evening." She said.

"Do you think he'll be excited?" Gabby asked, still jumping up and down like a nut.

"Girl, what is wrong with you, and yes, he is more than ready to have children. I just figured we would wait until after the wedding." Lu Lu laughed looking at Gabby.

"I'm happy! I can't stop thinking about you with your belly all poked out. And when the baby gets here, oooooohhhh, the baby. I'm just going to love her to death. Awwww, a little diva!" Gabby yelled.

"How do you know it will be a girl?" Lu Lu asked.

"I just do. Our first baby has to be a girl!" Gabby laughed.

"Oh, 'our', first baby?"

"Yes, she will be all of ours, you know that...You know how we do!" She responded.

"You guys are crazy!" we all laughed and hugged our new mommy to be.

I'm so proud of Lu Lu. She's come a long way. She has learned how to love. I've never seen her this way with anybody but us. My baby has grown up. I get teary eyed just thinking about it.

If she has a girl, our men are definitely in trouble. They will have one spoiled little lady on there hands.

One more, ***True Diva.***

Vince

Lu Lu is on the way over here for dinner. She is a mess. I can tell something is wrong with her by the tone of her voice, but each time I ask, she says it's nothing.

I'm quite sure she is coming to tell me she is pregnant. I knew the moment after we made love. It was different from every other time. I could just tell.

I know it sounds crazy, but when I came, it took something out of me. Like I said, it was just different. But when she didn't mention anything the next month, I assumed I was wrong.

But lately, I've been a mess. When I was in Africa, I thought I had the flu...but I only felt bad in the morning. I can't eat, I'm throwing up, I feel week, and then miraculously, by the afternoon I feel fine.

You know how men are. When they are feeling bad, the first thing they do (if they are single) is call mommy. I called my mom's all the way from Africa to whine like a baby. She told me to hush, and then said it...

"Boy, Lu Lu must be pregnant. You need to call and check on her".

So I did. But when I called, she was fine. She had so much energy; I wished she could have sent me some via e-mail.

My gut tells me I'm right though. I can't wait for her to get here. I've been sitting in the front room window for 10 minutes waiting. I'm ready. I told her I didn't want to be fifty years old having my first child, so this would be perfect. I'm thirty-three years old. It's time. And this woman will be my wife in two and a half weeks.

"Finally" I yelled as I ran to the front door. I had to pause and pull myself together. I didn't want her to know I was waiting at the door like a puppy.

"Hey babe, how you doing? What took so long?" I asked. "It only took me fifteen minutes to get here Vincent." She laughed. "I saw you peaking out the blinds. Did Boo Boo miss mommy?" She laughed.

I had to laugh too. I thought I was being all sneaky. She knows me too well for that though. But enough chit chat, I need to know what's going on.

"So?" I asked.

"So, what?" She asked with her brow furrowed as if I was crazy.

"Don't you have something to tell me? That is what you said." I asked impatiently.

"Well damn Vince, can't I get in the front door good baby. I brought dinner, here take these bags. Can't we relax and eat. Stop acting like a **BAYBIE**." She said emphasizing the word.

Yep, I knew it! Woo hoo! Okay, I gotta pull myself together until she actually tells me something.

"Oh sorry babe. Let me take this stuff." I said. I went into the kitchen and made our plates.

As Lu walked into the room, her eyes got as big as saucers, she turned pale, put her hand over her mouth and ran into the bathroom.

I ran in behind her. I got her a warm wash cloth as she puked her guts out. This girl puked until she start dry heaving. While I felt sorry for her in that condition, I couldn't help but be excited.

"So, does this mean I'm going to be a daddy?" I smiled behind her.

"Y, y, yes". She said between dry heaves. Then she started to cry. It's a shame she has to go through all of this. Poor thing, I thought as I handed her the face towel.

"Vince!" Lu yelled from the bathroom. "Please take that Chinese food outside. If I smell it again, I'm liable to throw up all my intestines, that's the only thing left!"

"Alright!" I yelled back. I was cheesing from ear to ear. My chest was poked out a little further than usual.

As I walked outside to the trashcan, I grabbed my cell. I had to call my boys and tell them my new name is Big Daddy!

Malcolm

"Hello?" I said rolling over Gabby to answer the phone. We were watching that movie "Ray". Jamie Foxx is a talented brotha. I'm glad the won the Oscar for this one. He truly deserved it. Heck, I almost started crying on this one.

"Hey Malcolm, what up dog?" Vince said.

"Nuttin' much dog. Sittin' here laid up with Gabriel. What up?" I asked.

"Man, whose da man?" He asked.

"Dog, what are you talking about?" I laughed.

"Man, just call me Bid Daddy!" He yelled.

"Congratulations man, you know Gabby told me. I just didn't want to ruin the surprise for ya bro!" I laughed.

"Man, I'm so happy I can't even see straight! You go back to your girl, I'll holla back!" He yelled into the phone.

"Alright man, peace." I said as I laughed at him.

"Who was that, Vince?" Gabby laughed. "I could hear his loud behind all the way over here. He is really happy isn't he?" She asked.

"Yep, the brotha is on cloud nine baby." I said.

"That's wonderful". She smiled. "I can't wait for her to get here, new babies smell so good. I just know she is going to be beautiful."

"And just how do you know the baby will be a she?" I asked.

"I just know. I've been dreaming about this beautiful little girl for about three or four months now....I didn't know whose she was, but I knew it was someone close. I know exactly what their little girl is going to look like." She dazed off.

"Really?"

"Yep, I do."

"Well, I can't wait until she has the baby either. You know how I feel about kids."

"No, actually I don't. We never had that conversation." She said.

"I love them. That's why I work in the ped's unit. I've just been waiting on the right woman to have them with. But now I found her." I smiled.

"I can't wait to have our first child, but I don't want anymore than two."

"I'm with you when you are right. It will be hard enough raising kids in this day and age. We don't need five and six of them running around."

"Well, I'm glad we agree on that." She smiled as she kissed me on the lips.

"Uh hu, we are not married. I'm waiting for my wedding night!" I said as she began to undress me.

"Whatever Malcolm!" She laughed as she stopped trying to undress me.

"That didn't mean stop. No means yes tonight baby!" I said as I pulled her close to me.

I love this woman....

The Wedding Day
Deja

As Lu Lu marched down the aisle, I tilted my head and just gazed at her. She looked so beautiful. There was a peaceful look on her face that she never seemed to have before. I began to cry, and so did she. I looked over at Gabby, and she grabbed my arm as she cried like a baby.

Lu was marching to that song "We Must be in Love" by Pure Soul. As she sway from side to side, step by step, we cried even harder. I was so happy for my sister, and my new brother Vince. His eyes were flooded. He loves her so much.

My own wedding day was becoming more of a reality. I never thought this would happen, not in a million years. When I married David, Lord rest his soul, I thought that was it.

I've always loved Derrick, always. I just never thought it was possible. At this moment, I am happier than I've ever been.

"Thank you Lord!"

David's home going services went smoothly, and his son is truly beautiful. It broke my heart when I held him. I began to weep the instant I picked him up. He clutched his little hand on to my blouse, and I cried harder. It crushed my heart to know someone so tiny, innocent, and beautiful will never know his father.

Although our marriage was a failure, David was a good man. I created a scrap book for the baby. It was a collection of pictures, certificates, and all other kinds of mementos of David. I tried to create a time line of life events so his son will have some sort of grasp on the magnificent and successful man his father was. Sandy broke down when I gave it to her.

It felt good to close that chapter once and for all. Although David still speaks to me. I know it may sound crazy to some, but he visits me from time to time. The last time he appeared, he apologized and told me how happy he was for Derrick and me. He told me Derrick was a good man, and that he could rest peacefully knowing I was with him.

That night I prayed like never before. After David came to me, I had no second thoughts about my marriage to Derrick. I thanked the Lord for sparing my life, and giving me a new one.

I tried to tell my girls, but they said it was most likely a dream. But I know it was real.

I glanced over at my man, my future husband. He was cheesing from ear to ear watching Lu walk down that aisle. He glanced back at me with the warmest, most comforting smile. I truly love him.

I am blessed, thank you Lord!

Gabby

The music began to play, and I just knew that I would lose it. When Lu Lu stepped into the door way, she was breath taking. I grabbed Deja's arm, and we both began to cry. I was so glad she suggested we hide tissue in our bouquets. If not, I would have been a mess.

I looked over at Malcolm and smiled. He winked and blew me a kiss. Everyone look so beautiful.

As Pure Soul harmonized and Lu walked down the aisle, my own wedding became more of reality. I still can't believe we are all going to be married, but it is slowly but surely happening.

About a week ago, I was telling Malcolm how I hoped everything went okay with our wedding. I made my usual "just my luck" comment, but before I could finish I felt his hand over my mouth.

"Gabriel, are you a Christian woman?" He asked.

"Yes, of course?" I answered confused.

"Then you know he doesn't make mistakes, and there's no such thing as luck. He brought us together, and no 'man' can tear us apart. So please, Gabby, please stop waiting for something to go wrong. Don't let the devil do that to you, better yet, don't let the devil do that to us!" He said. Then he kissed me.

You know, I never quite thought about it that way. All these years, I've been allowing the devil to creep in while I second guess God. The all knowing.

However, today, I stand before everyone a convicted woman. I stand on faith and God's promises to me as a Christian. He will never leave nor forsake me. And he will never give me more than I can handle.

As I look back on my life, I've never experienced anything bad enough to make me such a worry wart, I guess the devil had a strong hold on my courage and my faith, but no more.

"I rebuke you devil, in the name of Jesus, get under my feet!"

Lu Lu

The minute I stepped foot in the sanctuary, I began to cry. It was all so overwhelming. Vince looked at me with a look I've never seen before. He was so handsome in that tux, I couldn't believe my eyes. And my girls, they looked so beautiful.

They were a mess though, they were boo hooing so hard, it made me cry even harder. And their men are just as bad. Once glance in Malcolm and Derrick's direction, and they were cheesing from ear to ear with tears in their eyes.

Lord, I thought this day wasn't possible. I never thought I would be capable of loving any man this freely. My heart

was as cold as ice. I had even given up on the possibility of children, but at this moment I am carrying a life inside of me. A blessing from the Lord God Almighty. A part of the man I love.

When I was a little girl, I served on the church drill team. We each had our own Bible verse. My verse was *Proverbs 3:5 - 6* "Trust in the Lord with all thine heart, and lean not into thine own understanding. In all thy ways acknowledge him, and he shall direct thy paths". I've always loved that verse, but I obviously wasn't abiding by it. But that is no longer true. As of this moment, I am trusting in the Lord, and living on faith alone.

I began to pray silently, "Lord, I don't understand everything that is happening in my life, but I'm asking you to lead me."

Then I looked at my Pastor, next at Vincent, and I said, "I do!"

Certified Diva

All of you artificially flavored Divas
Jump back and slap yourselves
Are you a Diva
You don't even know what a Diva is

You think it's all about the dress
Fresh from head to toe
Think it's about up-doo's
And stilettos

OH NO
Baby you're confused
It's more than hair weave
And ran over shoes

See, Divas aren't made
Divas are re-birthed
Divanistic from the new womb
Until she is one with the earth

Sassy but so classy
She only speaks truth
Divas don't have time
To play games with you

Diva is about her business
No matter what it is

From standing in the board room
To raising her kids

Diva is not your cheering section
She won't just go along with what you say
If your wrong, she'll say your wrong
And set your crooked ways straight

Diva treats her man like a King
Cause she won't accept anything less
So paupers get your head straight
And check your breath

Don't worry about being shot down
Diva is very kind
Shut your game down wit a smile
So sweet you won't even mind

Cause Diva is not evil
Her nose is not stuck in the up position
She treats folks how she likes to be treated
And always has the best of intentions

Loyal to the end
Always making time for her friends
She's that shoulder to cry on
And never misuses or abuses personal information

So Ms. Artificial
if Divanism is what you want to do
The first step you should take
Is to change you

Clean up your house and your mind
Take care of your soul
I ask you again are you a Diva
A Diva would know

Meet the Author

Lena Middleton is a graduate of the
University of Indianapolis.
She currently resides in Indianapolis, IN with her husband
and two children.